CULTURES OF THE WORLD

Monaco

Cavendish Square
New York

Published in 2022 by Cavendish Square Publishing, LLC
243 5th Avenue, Suite 136, New York, NY 10016
Copyright © 2022 by Cavendish Square Publishing, LLC

Third Edition

Website: cavendishsq.com

This publication represents the opinions and views of the author based on his or her personal experience, knowledge, and research. The information in this book serves as a general guide only. The author and publisher have used their best efforts in preparing this book and disclaim liability rising directly or indirectly from the use and application of this book.

All websites were available and accurate when this book was sent to press.

Library of Congress Cataloging-in-Publication Data

Names: King, David C., author. | Keppeler, Jill, author.
Title: Monaco / David C. King and Jill Keppeler.
Description: Third edition. | New York : Cavendish Square Publishing,
   [2022] | Series: Cultures of the world | Includes bibliographical
   references and index.
Identifiers: LCCN 2021013909 | ISBN 9781502662699 (library binding) | ISBN
   9781502662705 (ebook)
Subjects: LCSH: Monaco--Juvenile literature.
Classification: LCC DC945 .K54 2022 | DDC 944.9/49--dc23
LC record available at https://lccn.loc.gov/2021013909

Writers: David C. King; Jill Keppeler, third edition
Editor, third edition: Jill Keppeler
Designer, third edition: Jessica Nevins

PICTURE CREDITS
The photographs in this book are used with the permission of: Cover Djordje Ognjanovic/Shutterstock.com; p. 1 Richard Cummins/Lonely Planet Images/Getty Images Plus; pp. 3, 63 Romeo Reidl/Moment/Getty Images Plus; pp. 5, 122 SbytovaMN/iStock/Getty Images Plus; p. 6 khomyakov/iStock/Getty Images Plus; p. 7 Damiano Mariotti/Shutterstock.com; pp. 8, 46, 56, 60, 102, 116, 119 VALERY HACHE/AFP via Getty Images; p. 10 Zloyel/iStock/Getty Images Plus; p. 12 kosmozoo/DigitalVision Vectors/Getty Images; p. 13 artherng/RooM/Getty Images; p. 14 SI Imaging Services/Imazins/Getty Images; p. 15 bwzenith/iStock Editorial/Getty Images Plus; pp. 17, 20 Catalin Daniel Ciolca/iStock Editorial/Getty Images Plus; p. 18 Glenn van der Knijff/Lonely Planet Images/Getty Images Plus; p. 22 Henningstad/iStock/Getty Images Plus; p. 24 bparren/iStock/Getty Images Plus; p. 25 Sepia Times/Universal Images Group via Getty Images; pp. 27, 77 eugenesergeev/iStock Editorial/Getty Images Plus; p. 29 Christian SAPPA/Gamma-Rapho via Getty Images; p. 31 Universal History Archive/Universal Images Group via Getty Images; p. 32 Keystone-France/Gamma-Rapho via Getty Images; pp. 33, 70 work by Lisa Kling/Moment/Getty Images Plus; p. 35 Thomas D. McAvoy/The LIFE Picture Collection via Getty Images; p. 36 PLS Pool/Getty Images; p. 38 BORIS HORVAT/AFP via Getty Images; pp. 40, 51 Education Images/Universal Images Group via Getty Images; p. 43 Peter Phipp/Photolibrary/Getty Images Plus; pp. 44, 128 Patrice Coppee/The Image Bank/Getty Images Plus; p. 48 Kristine Demirtchian/EyeEm/Getty Images; p. 53 SvetlanaSF/iStock Editorial/Getty Images Plus; p. 54 AndreaAstes/iStock Editorial/Getty Images Plus; pp. 58, 78 Ceri Breeze/iStock Editorial/Getty Images Plus; p. 62 Patrick Aventurier/Getty Images; p. 65 Atlantide Phototravel/The Image Bank Unreleased/Getty Images; p. 66 Ikonya/iStock/Getty Images Plus; p. 68 Oleh_Slobodeniuk/E+/Getty Images; pp. 73, 100 michel Setboun/The Image Bank Unreleased/Getty Images; p. 74 mariusz_prusaczyk/iStock Editorial/Getty Images Plus; p. 76 John Greim/The Image Bank/Getty Images Plus; p. 80 Veronica Garbutt/Lonely Planet Images/Getty Images Plus; p. 82 Dennis Macdonald/Photolibrary/Getty Images Plus; p. 85 FAG/Shutterstock.com; p. 86 Thierry Orban/Getty Images; p. 87 Kalim Saliba/Moment/Getty Images; p. 90 Stefanos Tsitsipas/EyeEm/Getty Images; p. 92 Catherine Leblanc/Godong/Stone/Getty Images; p. 94 John Borthwick/Lonely Planet Images/Getty Images Plus; pp. 96, 109 YANN COATSALIOU/AFP via Getty Images; p. 98 User10095428_39/iStock Editorial/Getty Images Plus; p. 99 Michael Mulkens/iStock Editorial/Getty Images Plus; p. 101 Roka/Shutterstock.com; p. 104 binabina/iStock/Getty Images Plus; p. 106 SbytovaMN/iStock/Getty Images Plus; p. 107 Neil Massey/The Image Bank/Getty Images Plus; p. 110 Andrew Hetherington/The Image Bank/Getty Images Plus; p. 112 saiko3p/iStock Editorial/Getty Images Plus; p. 113 Sven Jacobsen/Stone/Getty Images Plus; p. 114 SC Pool - Corbis/Corbis via Getty Images; p. 117 Westend61/Getty Images; p. 120 Pascal Le Segretain/Getty Images; p. 124 bensib/iStock Editorial/Getty Images Plus; p. 126 Vladimir Mironov/iStock/Getty Images Plus; p. 127 Vitalii Kholmohorov/iStock/Getty Images Plus; p. 130 Oksana Mizina/Shutterstock.com; p. 131 Brent Hofacker/Shutterstock.com.

Some of the images in this book illustrate individuals who are models. The depictions do not imply actual situations or events.

CPSIA compliance information: Batch #CS22CSQ: For further information contact Cavendish Square Publishing LLC, New York, New York, at 1-877-980-4450.

Printed in the United States of America

CONTENTS

MONACO TODAY

MONACO IS UNIQUE. THIS SOVEREIGN CITY-STATE ALONG THE Mediterranean Sea, bordered by France and near Italy, is the second-smallest country in the world, larger than only Vatican City. In fact, its relatively tiny 0.8 square miles (2 square kilometers) could fit into New York City's Central Park with a good deal of room to spare. Its population, while dense, is smaller than that of any U.S. state or territory.

Don't judge Monaco solely by its size, however. The city-state is one of the most luxurious tourist destinations in the world, with more millionaires per capita than anywhere else. It is known for its gambling in the legendary Monte Carlo area, its famous Grand Prix Formula One race, and much more.

For all its glitz and glamour, its history dates back to the Stone Age, with evidence of early human habitation preserved in its museums. It also has a legendary connection to Greek mythology, and its monarchy, which has medieval roots, is one of the oldest in the region.

While the residents of this famous city-state do face some of the same problems as the rest of the world, including climate change, even many of Monaco's issues tend

Monaco is less than a square mile, but it runs from the sea to the mountains.

to be unique. Let's take a look at this sparkling, wealthy city-state and what makes it so different from other places in our world.

TOURISM

One of Monaco's main industries is tourism—and a very successful industry it is. While it is one of the most expensive places in the world, more than 7 million people visit it each year. It is known for its beaches and its boating, thanks to its location in the middle of the French Riviera, part of the Mediterranean coastline. The climate, with warm summers and mild winters, certainly does not hurt.

People also visit for its car races. The famous Grand Prix has taken place on a twisty, turning route right in the city-state's streets almost every year since 1929, although it was canceled in 2020 due to the COVID-19 pandemic. Museums, gardens, and festivals are also a draw, as is the ornate royal palace, built in the 13th century.

Monaco's other main draw is its casinos. The first one, the Casino de Monte-Carlo, opened in 1863 and has profoundly affected the fortunes of the city-state and its ruling family. However, Monaco's own residents are not allowed to gamble.

GOVERNMENT

Monaco has a constitutional monarchy, which is a governmental system in which a country is governed by a monarch whose power is limited by a constitution. It is currently ruled by Prince Albert II, who took the throne in 2005. His family—the Grimaldi family—has held power there on and off since the 13th century.

Monaco has had a constitution since 1911, although it was revised in 1962. The city-state has one legislative house, the National Council, which has 24 elected members. It has to approve all laws. Monaco also has a Supreme Court that is the highest judicial authority in the city-state.

Monaco had been a member of the United Nations (UN) since 1993. It is not a member of the European Union (EU), but it does use the euro as currency.

Monaco's small area holds many residents and many tourists.

CULTURE

The culture of Monaco is a mix of many things. It is strongly influenced by nearby France and Italy; in fact, more than 25 percent of the population is French, followed by Italians, Swiss, and Belgians. The citizens of Monaco, called Monegasques, make up only about one-fifth of the population of about 38,000.

Monaco's population is very wealthy. Nearly a third of its residents are millionaires, and its GDP per capita is more than $165,000, one of the highest in the world. None of the population lives below the poverty line. The population is also quite religious. More than 90 percent of Monaco residents are Roman Catholic, the official religion. However, the constitution does guarantee freedom of worship.

The Grimaldi family has had a strong impact on Monaco's culture over the centuries it has been in their control. The royal family has supported the arts and sciences, as well as many charities.

LANGUAGE

Because of longstanding ties between Monaco and France (and the hefty French population), the official language of Monaco is French. However, the people of Monaco also speak Italian, English, and Monegasque. The latter language is a dialect of Ligurian, from Liguria, a region in Italy, and it has much in common

Prince Albert II is the current ruler of Monaco. He married Charlene Wittstock in 2011.

with Italian. While it once was a language that was only spoken, in the past 100 years, Monaco natives started turning it into a written language. It was nearly extinct in the 1970s, but today, the children of Monaco learn Monegasque in public primary schools. It also appears, with French, on some street signs.

In the early 21st century, Monaco dealt with a number of changes, including the succession from Prince Rainier III (who had ruled for 56 years) to his son, Albert II. There was also criticism from other countries about its loose regulations on banking. However, there were also bright spots, including the launch of the city-state's first satellite in 2020. Also, as of 2002, thanks to a new treaty between Monaco and France, the city-state will not revert to France even if the Grimaldi family has no direct male heirs.

As Monaco moves further into the 21st century, there are more bright spots ahead. Its residents have the greatest life expectancy in the world, and the economy of Monaco is still going strong. There is no doubt that challenges lie ahead, too, but the city-state is prepared to meet them.

GEOGRAPHY

The Mediterranean Sea is a key part
of Monaco's geography.

1

MONACO'S LOCATION—RIGHT ON the Mediterranean Sea, in the middle of the French Riviera—is important to the city-state's history, economy, and culture. As with some other aspects of the area, its geography is a study in extremes, from sea level at the Mediterranean rising to the foothills of the Alps. This small space is packed with homes, businesses, and other buildings, as its population of about 38,000 people makes it one of the most densely populated countries in the world—and that does not even count the many tourists who visit Monaco every year. The city-state is entirely urban.

Monaco's climate is a very important aspect of its geography. It has the classic Mediterranean climate: warm and sunny in the summer and wet and mild in the winter. This helps draw tourists to its luxurious resorts and beaches. The average temperature year-round is 61 degrees Fahrenheit (16 degrees Celsius) with only about 60 days of rainfall in the average year.

Monaco's official name is the Principality of Monaco, or Principauté de Monaco in French.

The temperature ranges from an average of 50°F (10°C) in January to 75°F (24°C) in August.

QUARTIERS

Monaco has four traditional *quartiers*, or sections, although the city-state is generally considered to have five quartiers now. The original quartiers are Monaco-Ville, La Condamine, Monte Carlo, and Fontvieille. Moneghetti, a suburb once part of La Condamine, is considered the fifth quartier today. Monaco is further divided into 10 wards, with another one planned, and 173 city blocks.

The oldest part of the city-state is Monaco-Ville, called the old city, situated on the Rock of Monaco. The Rock is a steep-sided finger of land that is flat on top and extends 2,600 feet (793 meters) into the Mediterranean Sea. From almost any point on this promontory, there are breathtaking views of the sea and the entire Principality of Monaco.

A very steep, red brick pedestrian pathway called Rampe Major, built in the 1500s, connects the port area to the palace on top of the Rock of Monaco. The maze of narrow, twisting streets and covered walkways is crowded with villas, apartment buildings, and the shops of Old Town. This picturesque area, with modern buildings challenging ancient structures that were built hundreds of years ago, also contains public gardens, several museums, and the majestic Cathedral of Monaco.

La Condamine is the area around Monaco's main port. It can be reached from the top of the Rock by the Rampe Major or by the most unusual feature of Monaco's transportation system: a number of escalators and elevators

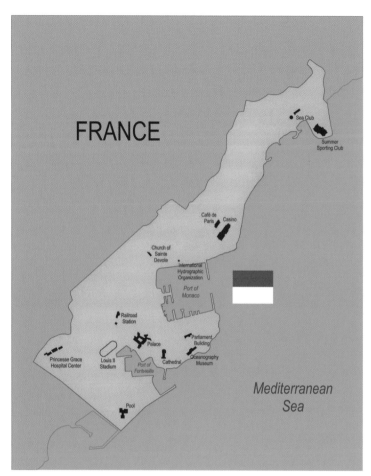

Monaco packs a lot into a small space, including sporting facilities, casinos, and ports. The main port of Monaco is also known as Port Hercules.

(called lifts) that connect the steepest streets. La Condamine is a shopping and commercial center with a promenade along the harbor, where visitors can gaze at the dazzling array of cruise ships and luxury yachts.

The original port of Monaco, Port Hercules, is located at La Condamine. To the southwest of Port Hercules (on the other side of the Rock) is a smaller and newer harbor, the Port of Fontvieille. Between 1966 and 1973, an ambitious landfill project reclaimed 74 acres (30 hectares) of land from the sea, pushing the southernmost region of Monaco into the Mediterranean and forming a new harbor.

Fontvieille is relatively new compared to most of the other quartiers, built on this reclaimed land from the sea in the 1970s. It is home to a number of Monaco's light industries, the port, some residential areas, and a sports stadium.

This view shows part of La Condamine and Monte Carlo, as well as part of Port Hercules.

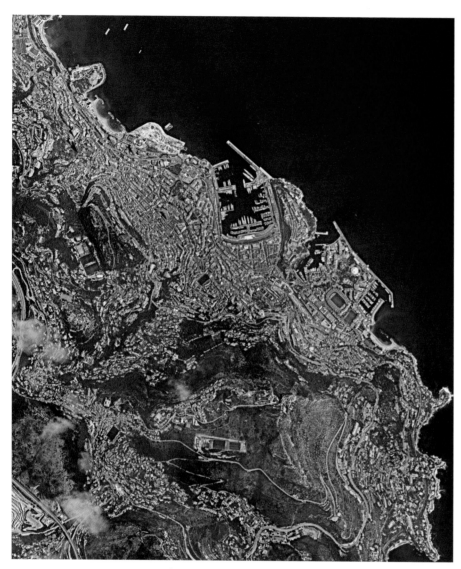

This area also has a number of museums, including the Naval Museum.

In addition, Fontvieille has many parks and a spectacular rose garden. More than 4,000 rose plants form the Princess Grace Rose Garden, which was planted in honor of one of Monaco's most beloved princesses, the late Princess Grace, who married Prince Rainier III in 1956. The rose garden adjoins other exotic gardens in Parc Fontvieille, including a coastal path called Chemin des Sculptures (Sculpture Road), which is lined with contemporary sculptures.

Monte Carlo is probably the most famous of Monaco's areas. In fact, many outsiders assume that the area of Monte Carlo is Monaco itself. The most famous part of the region is the Place du Casino and the Square Beaumarchais. The great gambling casino and some of Europe's most elegant hotels and restaurants have made this a gathering place for royalty and millionaires for more than a century. In the 21st century, Monte Carlo has drawn the most famous names in sports and entertainment. There are few places in the world that can match the extravagant lifestyle that Monte Carlo displays.

This satellite overview of Monaco clearly shows the ports of the city-state.

Many of the region's 19th-century villas are being replaced by high-rise apartments—so much so that people jokingly call Monte Carlo the "New York on the Mediterranean" because of its skyline of tall buildings. In spite of the intrusion of modern high-rise buildings, Monte Carlo retains a spectacular display of architectural styles, some dating back to the 14th and 15th centuries. Another beautiful feature of this region is the terracing of the steep hills. There are also numerous gardens that surround the casino with bright colors and greenery.

This photo shows the façade of the Monte Carlo Casino in 2019.

THE WARDS OF MONACO

Monaco is only one municipality, and a small one at that, but it is still divided into 10 distinct wards. Four have the same names as the original quartiers: Monte Carlo, Monaco-Ville, Fontvieille, and La Condamine. The others are La Rousse, Larvotto, La Colle, Les Révoires, Moneghetti, and Saint Michel. Each has its own personality and character, from the more residential to the more industrial, and its own attractions for visitors. For example, Larvotto has the Avenue Princesse Grace, with its extremely pricey real estate, while La Colle contains many businesses. Les Révoires has the highest point in Monaco, 459 feet (140 m) above sea level on the pathway called Chemin des Révoires, on the slopes of Mont Agel. In addition, Le Portier will be a new area in Monaco, due to be completed in 2025.

Building styles in Monaco must take the city-state's unique geography into account.

To the northeast of Monte Carlo is the ward known as Larvotto, which has Monaco's only beach area. It has both public and private sections. In the private section, bathers can rent cushioned lounges and colorful parasols. The last major construction project by Prince Rainier III was the Grimaldi Forum Monaco, which was completed in 2000, and it is also found in Larvotto. The forum is used as a conference center and also houses art exhibits, cultural center ballets, operas, and dance performances.

Monaco's fifth quartier is Moneghetti, a unique area on the western edge of the country that features an exotic garden of tropical and subtropical plants including cacti and other succulent plants. The Mediterranean climate allows the plants to survive farther north than they usually would. The Jardin Exotique (Exotic Garden) is more than 161,000 square feet (14,957 sq m) and was constructed by terracing the sheer cliffs, a task that took 20 years. The terraced gardens are connected by footbridges, and secluded spots are formed by dense foliage. It is one of Monaco's most popular tourist destinations, thanks in part to its beautiful views.

Near the foot of the Exotic Garden cliff is the Observatory Cave, which has an entrance about 328 feet (100 m) above sea level. Visitors climb down about 300 steps (most of which are slippery) inside the cliffside, where they enter a series of caves naturally decorated with countless stalagmites and stalactites.

It is warm in the cave—which is, in fact, one of the warmest in Europe—and very humid. Some caves feature ice-blue pools and natural sculptures. The largest cave resembles a cathedral, complete with rock pillars and rock sculptures. As in all the caves, there is an eerie silence except for the gentle sound of dripping water.

The Observatory Cave lies below the Jardin Exotique.

Because pretty much all of Monaco is urban, there's not much wildlife or wild plants. What there is by the way of plants has generally been planted on purpose.

The most remarkable features of the caves are some prehistoric rock drawings that are among the oldest in the world. Scientists estimate that the "rock scratches" may have been made hundreds of thousands of years ago. The scenes depict prehistoric animals, including early reindeer. The cave complex is also home to the Museum of Prehistoric Anthropology, with displays of human evolution, as well as the bones of reindeer, mammoths, and hippopotamuses.

PLANT AND ANIMAL LIFE

Monaco has very little in the way of natural flora and fauna. In fact, in terms of wildlife, Monaco has fewer than 30 species of amphibians, birds, mammals, and reptiles that are native to the city-state. However, there are many sea animals in the waters of the Mediterranean, including striped and Atlantic dolphins and several types of whales.

Land animals tend to be small, with the roe deer and the red fox being two of the larger. For all its limited wildlife, Monaco has three national animals—the European hedgehog, the European rabbit, and the wood mouse.

Monaco has more native plant species, but there are few plants growing wild. It has typical Mediterranean plants such as palms, aloes, carobs, and others. There are also a number of wildflowers, including lilies, roses, and bell-like flowers called fritillarias. While there are few wild plants, there are many gardens—some quite elaborate.

Le Jardin Exotique, for example, on the steep cliff face near the caves, was started in 1933 with several thousand succulents and cacti planted in crevices and on ledges within the sheer rock wall. Since then, roughly 2,000 more exotic plants have been added. Winding paths and flimsy-looking footbridges connect different sections; some bridges hang precariously above African candelabra cacti, which grow to heights of more than 30 feet (9 m). Another towering cactus is the Moroccan euphorbia, which reaches 50 feet (15 m). A favorite among visitors is the Mexican echino cactus, which looks like a guinea pig with sharp spikes and is popularly known as a "mother-in-law's pillow." For those who dare to look up while traversing the bridges, the garden offers spectacular views of the harbor, the Mediterranean, and part of the French Riviera.

Another popular garden is the Jardin Japonais (Japanese Garden). It was built to offer a corner of quiet and peace, and it was blessed by a Shinto priest. Visitors are encouraged to use the garden for meditation and contemplation.

Two beautiful gardens grace the heights of Monte Carlo. The Jardins du Casino (Casino Gardens) surround the casino with bright splashes of color, and additional interest is provided by changing art exhibits along the center pathway.

Nearby, just outside the cathedral, is the exotic Jardins Saint Martin (Saint Martin Gardens). Aleppo pines and yellow agaves cover terraces that wind

around the Rock of Monaco. Scattered through the greenery are medieval fortifications and turrets built in the 1700s. As with all of Monaco's gardens, these are perfectly tended by teams of gardeners dressed in uniform.

WILDLIFE ON VIEW

While there are few native animals, Monaco has some intriguing opportunities for viewing wildlife. The Zoological Gardens were established by Prince Rainier III and are one of the last royal menageries in the world. There, about 250 animals representing 50 species live—at least temporarily. They were all either donated, abandoned, or taken by Monaco's customs authority, and they eventually move on to zoos in other countries.

The most famous wildlife-viewing area, however, is probably the Musée Océanographique (Oceanographic Museum). It was built by Prince Albert I in 1910 as a "temple of the sea." The aquarium is regarded as one of the most outstanding in the world, and its many tanks are used for research as well as to display marine life. There are thousands of species on display. The famous marine explorer Jacques-Yves Cousteau was director of the museum for 30 years, until 1988.

Monaco is very involved in the conservation of its plants and animals. Prince Albert I was a noted oceanographer and pioneer in environmental conservation. Prince Albert II created the Prince Albert II of Monaco Foundation in part to protect the environment, and he continues to speak about and work toward the city-state's commitment to conservation today.

INTERNET LINKS

www.informationfrance.com/monaco/
Learn more about the quartiers of Monaco.

www.lonelyplanet.com/monaco/attractions/musee-oceanographique-de-monaco/a/poi-sig/1188681/359266
This Lonely Planet page tells about the Musée Océanographique, including some of its history and its attractions.

www.visitmonaco.com/en/place/the-gardens/93/zoological-gardens
This tourist website provides information on the Zoological Gardens as well as other sites in Monaco.

HISTORY

Monaco's history dates back to the Stone Age. People have fought over this small slice of land for thousands of years.

MONACO'S HISTORY, LIKE THAT OF many countries, has been heavily influenced by its location. Its spot on the shores of the Mediterranean Sea offered a place for a harbor and access to trading routes, and the Rock of Monaco was a solid defensive point.

2

Monaco also exists in the shadow of two large, powerful neighbors: France and Italy. France has taken control of Monaco on several occasions, and in the 21st century it continues to be responsible for the defense of Monaco's independence and sovereignty.

Monaco's relations with Italy have been unusual because there was no unified nation of Italy until the mid-19th century. For a thousand years before unification, the peninsula was divided into competing city-states, including Genoa, Florence, Venice, and Naples. The struggles among these powers have frequently involved Monaco. The Grimaldi family, which has ruled Monaco for many centuries, are descendants of Genovese statesmen and were also one of Genoa's most powerful ruling families.

STONE AGE ORIGINS

The caves of Monaco and the coastal area around it provide evidence of the presence of early humans dating to 200,000 to 400,000 years ago. Stone Age hunters scratched pictures on the walls of a cave deep inside the Rock of Monaco. These drawings, which are among the oldest cave art in the world, are protected in Monaco's famous Cave Observatory.

The Rock of Monaco sits between the city-state's two ports today.

The coastal region around Monaco has provided evidence of Neanderthal hunters, who roamed the Mediterranean coast from about 90,000 BCE to 40,000 BCE. The first modern humans arrived around 30,000 BCE. They lived by hunting and gathering wild foods, then began growing crops around 6000 BCE. The caves display remarkable cave art (or petroglyphs) of bison, seals, deer, and other animals.

By about 1000 BCE, Monaco was part of a lively Mediterranean sea trade that involved civilizations from places such as Phoenicia and Greece in the east and Rome and Carthage in the west. The ancient Greeks established many coastal trading posts. One was probably set up at Monaco around 600 BCE, although the Phoenicians may have colonized the area before them.

Some historians believe that the name "Monaco" may have been derived from the name of that early Greek colony, Monoikos. This colony was probably located in the area that became Monaco, which included land between the Rock of Monaco and the border of Italy. This larger Monaco, which existed until 1848, was about nine times larger than the present principality. The Greeks introduced grapes and olives to this area, which was already famous for its lemon orchards.

Rome took control of the area near the end of the Gallic Wars, which was about 50 BCE. During the height of the Roman Empire, roads and aqueducts were built along the coast from Italy to Spain. The greater Monaco flourished under Roman rule, providing Rome with olive oil, wine, and lemons. After the fall of Rome in the 5th century CE, various Germanic tribes invaded the area. Monaco's history is quite turbulent and imprecise over the next 500 years or so. Gradually, the region came under the influence of Genoa, one of the ambitious Italian city-states.

The first residents of this area of greater Monaco were likely the Ligures, who came from an area that is now part of Italy.

Monaco has been an important part of the sea trade for thousands of years. This drawing shows ships there in 1873.

MONACO AND HERCULES

The name of an early Greek colony, Monoikos, may have come from the Greek for "single house." This may be a sign of Monaco's longstanding connection to the Greek hero and demigod Heracles (Roman "Hercules"), who was sometimes called "Heracles Monoikos" (meaning "Heracles alone"). Legend says that he passed through the area, and the main port of Monaco is still called Port Hercules (or Port Hercule). There was allegedly a temple built to him in the area as well, though none has been found. Some historians have said, however, that the stories of Heracles in the area may be rewritten stories of the early Phoenicians in the region.

RISE OF THE GRIMALDIS

Modern Monaco and its ruling family emerged from the political maneuverings and wars of Renaissance Italy. For several hundred years, the city-state of Genoa was one of the most powerful in Italy, vying for wealth and influence with Naples, Venice, and the Vatican. The Grimaldi family provided many of Genoa's political, religious, and military leaders.

Near the end of the 12th century, the Monaco area became a colony of Genoa. Members of a faction called the Ghibellines, led by Fulco del Cassello, started to build a fortress on the Rock on June 10, 1215. However, the Rock soon became a symbol of struggle between the Ghibellines and another faction, the Guelfs. This faction (including its allies, the Grimaldi family) was expelled from Genoa in 1269.

This event was soon to become a turning point for Monaco. In 1297, François Grimaldi hatched a plot to seize control of Monaco and then use it as a base of operations against the Ghibellines in Genoa itself.

On January 8, 1297, Grimaldi (called Il Malizia or "The Cunning"—or possibly, "The Malicious") went to the Ghibelline fortress on the Rock of Monaco with a small band of soldiers.

As the story goes, with his men hidden in a garden, he disguised himself as a Franciscan monk and knocked on the door in the fortress gate. When two soldiers answered, Grimaldi asked for a night's lodging. As soon as the soldiers

let him in, he drew a dagger from his robe and murdered them. Grimaldi and his men quickly gained control of the fortress and all of Monaco. This was the beginning of Grimaldi rule in Monaco—and to this day, the coat of arms of the Grimaldi family features two armed monks.

Over the next century, the Grimaldis lost and regained control of Monaco several times as the struggle for power among Italy's states continued. The first time was in 1301, but Charles I (son of François Grimaldi's cousin, who succeeded him) took back the Rock in 1331. There were a few other lapses as well. In 1419, the French ruling family gave Monaco to the Grimaldis. However, the family members did not start to use the title "prince" until 1659.

The site of the Prince's Palace in Monaco originally had a fortress built in 1191.

The Ghibellines and Guelfs were opposing political parties, of sorts, in Italy during the Middle Ages. The Guelfs supported the power of the Catholic pope, while the Ghibellines supported the Holy Roman emperors of Germany—although some other factors may have played a role in some places, including in Florence with a blood feud between two families. It was the emperor at the time who gave the Ghibellines the area of Monaco as a colony, and this strife led to the expulsion of the Guelfs (and the Grimaldis) from Genoa in 1269. The feud (or some level of it) continued into the 14th century but faded soon after.

Because Monaco shares its borders with France, the Grimaldi princes have found it useful to maintain friendly relations with the French. However, for a little more than a century, from 1524 to 1641, Monaco was under the protection of Spain. Subsequently, in 1793, during the French Revolution, Monaco was annexed to France under the name "Fort Hercule." The turbulence of the Italian city-states was replaced by the turbulence of the French Revolution and the Napoleonic Wars that raged across Europe and the high seas from the 1790s to 1815.

The Congress of Vienna, a meeting of all the great powers of Europe, took place from 1814 to 1815. After this, the Grimaldis were returned to power, and Monaco was placed under the protection of Sardinia. Many members of the Grimaldi family had spent several years in prison during the upheaval of the French Revolution. When they were released, they had to sell most of their possessions in order to survive. In addition, the palace had been used as a warehouse and needed major repairs.

Even though the Grimaldis were once again the ruling family of Monaco, their problems were far from over. In 1848, the territories of Menton and Roquebrune revolted against Monaco's high taxes and demanded independence. These two areas had been part of the enlarged Monaco for hundreds of years, and their olives, oranges, and lemons had been Monaco's main source of income. When they gained independence, Monaco suddenly lost more than 90 percent of its land area and quickly became the poorest country in Europe. In 1861, Monaco signed a new treaty with France in which France again recognized

Monaco's independence and Monaco officially accepted the loss of Menton and Roquebrune. In 1865, a financial treaty was signed that involved customs duties and promised future cooperation between the two countries.

The Prince's Palace (shown here) was also used as a hospital during the French Revolution.

CASINOS AND WARTIME

Monaco still had many financial issues—but Princess Caroline, wife of Prince Florestan of Monaco, had an idea. She convinced first her husband and then, after he died in 1856, her son Charles III to raise money to build a casino in Monaco, one much like the Bad Homburg Casino in Germany.

It took some stops and starts, with different people running the casino and changes in location— as well as upgrades in transportation into Monaco—but the casino slowly started making money. The area was renamed Monte Carlo

RULERS OF MONACO

François Grimaldi
Rainier I
Charles I
Rainier II
Louis and Jean I, jointly
Louis
Jean I, Ambrose, and Antoine, jointly
Catalan
Claudine (under regency)
Lamberto
Jean II
Lucien
Honoré I
Charles II
Ercole

Honoré II, first to take the title of prince
Louis I
Antonio I
Louise Hippolyte (under regency)
Jacques I
Honoré III
French rulers from 1793 to 1814
Honoré IV
Honoré V
Florestan
Charles III
Albert I
Louis II
Rainer III
Albert II (current)

in Charles's honor. It was modeled after a famous gambling resort in Germany, which drew dazzling crowds of monarchs, dukes and duchesses, and other royalty, as well as Europe's wealthiest men and women. Prince Charles hired outstanding architects and designers to produce a remarkably ornate and rich style, with stained-glass skylights and windows, as well as enormous bronze lamps. Other luxurious buildings, such as the Hôtel de Paris and the Café de Paris, provided the wealthy and titled Europeans with reasons to plan excursions and vacations to Monte Carlo.

The casino provided the income source that Monaco desperately needed. By 1869, Prince Charles was able to do away with income taxes. The prince had been worried about the possible negative effects of gambling, so, from the beginning, citizens of Monaco have been forbidden to gamble in the casino.

With its economic base secure for the time being, the Grimaldi rulers could concentrate on other ways to modernize their little city-state. One of the most popular princes was Albert I (1848–1922). In 1911, after a peaceful revolution

with many protests by the people of Monaco, he gave Monaco a constitution that provided for limited participation in the government through an elected National Council. At the time, the National Council was granted almost no power beyond advising, but it was hailed as a step toward democracy.

Prince Albert I kept Monaco neutral during World War I (1914—1918), although the city-state did quietly help the Allies. As part of the Treaty of Versailles after the war, Monaco and France agreed that if the Grimaldi line died out, Monaco would become a state under French protection. The French army or navy could occupy Monaco, and Monaco had to ask France for permission for changes in the succession or alliances. The international policies of France and Monaco had to align.

This photo shows Prince Albert I of Monaco, who ruled the city-state through World War I.

This photo shows Prince Louis II of Monaco around 1930.

Like the rest of Europe, Monaco enjoyed the fast-paced life of the Roaring Twenties. American and European movie stars and famous athletes joined the parade of rich and famous people who vacationed in Monaco. The harbor became increasingly crowded with luxury yachts, and famous artists such as Pablo Picasso discovered the beauty of the beaches, with the sparkling Mediterranean and deep blue sky. In 1929, the first Grand Prix auto race brought together brilliantly colored race cars that roared around the sharp turns and steep hills of Monaco. The race quickly became one of Europe's premier sports events.

However, Monaco fell on hard times during the Great Depression of the 1930s. Because so much wealth was lost throughout Europe, revenues declined sharply at the casino and surrounding businesses.

Just as the world was beginning to recover from the Great Depression, it was plunged into World War II (1939—1945) because of the aggression of Nazi Germany, Fascist Italy, and militaristic Japan. The war years formed a dark chapter in Monaco's story. First, Prince Louis II (1870—1949) declared that Monaco would remain neutral, but he also supported the Vichy government, a regime set up in the southern half of France by Nazi Germany. Also, many residents of Monaco were Italian and supported Benito Mussolini's Fascist government.

This stance of Louis II created a deep rift between Louis and his grandson, Rainier III (1923—2005). Rainier spent the war years fighting with the French against Nazi Germany. Louis II, however, caved to pressure by Nazis to register the Jews living in Monaco, which started in July 1941. Things were a little more

complicated than they seemed: Louis II also allegedly used the Monaco police to warn Jewish people when the Nazi secret police were on their way.

Prince Rainier III was furious over reports that Jewish refugees, who were seeking to escape Nazi concentration camps, had mysteriously "disappeared" from Monaco's hotels. He blamed his grandfather's minister of state, Émile Roblot, for these actions and demanded his removal, but Louis refused. Many years later, in August 2015, Prince Albert II of Monaco (Prince Rainier III's son) officially apologized for his country's part in deporting Jews to Nazi camps during the war.

Monaco celebrates Liberation Day on September 3, marking the date in 1944 when the Allies (led by the United States) freed the city-state from the Axis Powers during World War II.

The wedding of Prince Rainier III and Grace Kelly in 1956 drew attention from around the globe. Not only was Kelly a famous American actress, she was also marrying into actual royalty, and it must have seemed like a fairy tale to many people. The couple had a private civil ceremony in the palace on April 18, 1956, followed by a huge gala at the Monaco Opera. Their church wedding took place the next day, with Kelly in a now-iconic white wedding gown and all the pomp a royal family can muster. More than 30 million viewers watched on live television. Their son, Prince Albert II, would later say in an interview that his parents considered the reaction to the wedding "overwhelming."

Supporters of Prince Louis insisted that he was at the mercy of Nazi power and had no choice but to give in to German demands. Despite his attempts at neutrality, however, the Italian army invaded Monaco in 1942, with the German army taking over in 1943. In September 1944, Monaco was liberated by the Allies.

MOVING INTO MODERN TIMES

Prince Rainier III succeeded his grandfather as the ruler of Monaco in 1949 and dominated the country's affairs for the next 56 years. He knew that the country needed a diversified economy. Monte Carlo could not provide enough revenue, especially after gambling casinos were opened in France and other countries. Through advertising and promotional campaigns, he transformed Monaco into a mecca for tourists, adding on to its luxurious facilities. Once a winter spa centered on gambling at Monte Carlo, Monaco now became a summer vacation spot as well, with an ambitious buildup of beach and harbor facilities.

Other building projects enabled Rainier to increase Monaco's boundaries. He doubled the port facilities, and the new land at Fontvieille made room for the construction of nonpolluting light industries. There were many reasons he was often called "the builder prince."

In 1955, Hollywood movie star Grace Kelly arrived in Monaco to shoot a film. She was introduced to the prince before a photo shoot at the palace.

Their whirlwind romance led to the "wedding of the century" one year later. The event captured the imagination of people everywhere.

Princess Grace never made another Hollywood film. Instead, she devoted herself to her royal duties. The image of the princess and the fairy tale wedding added luster to Monaco's appeal as a tourist center and glamorous destination. Throughout the next two decades, the yacht harbor, beaches, and hotels

The wedding of Prince Rainier III and Grace Kelly in 1956 captivated the world.

witnessed a steady procession of the rich and famous from around the world. The prince continued his building projects. One story says that this led Princess Grace to complain, jokingly, that people could not sunbathe on the beaches after 3 p.m. because of the shadow cast by Rainier's high-rise apartment buildings.

In 1982, Princess Grace died in an automobile accident on one of Monaco's notoriously steep roads. She apparently had suffered from a stroke while driving. The tragedy was a blow to the glamorous, fairy-tale atmosphere of the principality. In the years that followed, the royal image became tarnished by personal scandals involving the royal couple's three children—Caroline, Albert, and Stéphanie.

Early in 2000, Prince Rainier finished his last ambitious construction project: the Grimaldi Forum Monaco, a huge glass structure between Monte Carlo and the sea. The building is used for occasional art exhibitions in addition to business conferences. His hopes for a new project to build out farther into the Mediterranean, making use of Monaco's territorial waters, had to be put on hold when the 80-year-old prince's health began to fail. In March 2005, his son, Albert, took over the royal duties because his father was too ill to carry them out.

Prince Rainier died on April 6, 2005, and his son succeeded him as Prince Albert II of Monaco. On July 12, 2005, the formal accession took place. It included a solemn Mass at the cathedral where his father had been buried three months earlier.

In the years since Prince Albert took the throne, he has continued his father's building tradition as well as instituted a number of reforms. In July 2011, he married former Olympic swimmer Charlene Wittstock of South Africa. In December 2014, they had twins, Gabriella and Jacques, the latter of whom is the heir to the throne.

INTERNET LINKS

www.businessinsider.com/ap-monaco-seeks-forgiveness-for-deporting-jews-during-ww2-2015-8
This article details Prince Albert's apology for his country's role in deporting Jews during World War II.

www.townandcountrymag.com/society/tradition/a12787551/grace-kelly-wedding/
Read about the "wedding of the century" between Prince Rainier III and Grace Kelly, complete with vintage photos.

www.visitmonaco.com/en/place/museums/86/museum-of-prehistoric-anthropology
The website of the Museum of Prehistoric Anthropology in Monaco contains information on the museum's displays and archaeological digs in Monaco.

GOVERNMENT

The flag of Monaco has one band of white and one band of red. These colors have been used by the Grimaldis since about the 14th century.

TODAY, MONACO IS RULED BY A member of the same family that founded it back in 1297, more than 700 years ago. However, that rule has changed in many ways over the hundreds of years, and the prince no longer has absolute authority. A constitution (and a legislative house) limits his powers somewhat, and there is also a minister of state who helps run the government. Pierre Dartout has been Monaco's minister of state since September 2020.

In spite of the principality's lack of size and power, the government functions with great pageantry. The changing of the guard at the Prince's Palace, for example, is carried out with pomp and precision that is not unlike the changing of the guard at England's Buckingham Palace. Every day, large crowds gather outside the palace gates for the 11:55 a.m. ceremony. The 119 members of the Carabiniers du Prince (the prince's guards) put on an elaborate display of precision marching, with the sun glistening off their brilliant white summer uniforms and helmets. (Winter uniforms are deep blue with a red stripe.) There was a brief suspension of the public ceremony during the COVID-19 pandemic, although the ceremony did take place daily inside the palace.

The daily changing of the guard at the Prince's Palace is a big draw for tourists.

Other affairs of state have also involved colorful ceremonies. The 1956 marriage of Prince Rainier III and Hollywood film star Grace Kelly was memorable for its elaborate displays, including the bride's arrival in a harbor filled with yachts and boats, while a seaplane scattered red and white carnations across the water. The sky was filled with fireworks, while Monegasque and American flags parachuted down. Hundreds of guests filled the cathedral for the ceremony, while thousands more celebrated in the streets.

In 1997, Monaco celebrated 700 years of the Grimaldi dynasty, and in 2011, the city-state marked Prince Albert II's wedding to Charlene Wittstock. Once again, there were great displays of fireworks and noisy street celebrations, but the 1956 wedding continues to stand out as the principality's biggest fairy-tale moment.

BIG FISH, LITTLE FISH

France looms over Monaco as a gigantic force. In the event of a power struggle, French strength would easily swallow up the tiny city-state. Over the centuries, the Grimaldi princes have worked out agreements with their huge neighbor that have allowed Monaco to retain its independence. A treaty signed in 1861, for example, confirmed the principality's independence in exchange for accepting the loss of the regions of Menton and Roquebrune, which had rebelled in 1848 and were annexed by France.

There have been several other treaties to clarify relations. Under the terms of a treaty signed in 1918, if a royal prince dies without an heir, Monaco will become a state under French protection, with a number of checks on its power. In 2002, a new treaty specified that the city-state will pass to heirs in the female line even if there are no male heirs.

In the latter half of the 20th century, Monaco's insistence on having no income tax led to a serious dispute with France. Hundreds of wealthy French families established residences in Monaco to take advantage of the tax-free status. Several agreements were attempted, but people always found loopholes. When Prince Rainier III refused to impose taxes in 1962, President Charles de Gaulle of France responded by closing all the borders into Monaco. De Gaulle's action forced Prince Rainier to renegotiate and sign a new treaty with France in 1963. French citizens with less than five years' residence in Monaco would now be taxed at French rates. In addition, graduated taxes were imposed on Monegasque companies that conducted more than 25 percent of their business outside the principality.

Although France has a good deal of influence over Monaco, the principality continues to function as an independent nation. Monaco became a member of the United Nations in 1993 and has been active in several international bodies, including the European Organization for Security and Cooperation. The principality also has consulates in many European countries, as well as in the United States and Canada.

Monaco also goes its own way in financial matters. It did not become a member of the European Union, for example, instead preferring to maintain a customs union with France. This enables Monaco to use France's currency, which now happens to be the euro. Monaco even has the right to mint euro coins with Monegasque designs on one side.

The principality is determined to protect its liberal tax system and its confidentiality in banking rules that attract many foreign investors. In 2000, a French government report accused Monaco of lax policies regarding banking practices and taxes. The Monegasque government quickly investigated the claim and issued reports showing that nearly all the charges were inaccurate. However, in 2002, the Organisation for Economic Cooperation and Development (OECD) added Monaco to its blacklist for tax havens. The city-state was removed in 2009 after agreeing to follow rules. In 2018, OECD named Monaco as "compliant" with the organization's standards.

THE ROYAL FAMILY

Since the late 13th century, every prince of Monaco has been a member of the Grimaldi family. No other family in history has dominated a government for so long.

The family first became powerful in Genoa, one of several city-states that vied for power in Italy until the nation was finally unified in the 1860s. There were also times when the power struggles involved nearly all of Europe, including Spain and France. From time to time, the people of Monaco found themselves living under the protection of Spain, France, or even the kingdom of Sardinia in the early 1800s. Most of the time, however, the Grimaldis remained at the helm. The dynasty almost came to an end in 1731, when Prince Antoine I died without leaving a male heir. His daughter took over and ruled as princess, keeping the family line intact for her son.

Monaco was fortunate to have two fairly far-sighted rulers in the 19th and early 20th centuries. Prince Charles III negotiated the treaty of 1861 that guaranteed Monaco's independence, then built the fabled Monte Carlo Casino to provide both the family and the principality with income to offset the loss of Menton and Roquebrune.

Prince Charles III was succeeded by Prince Albert I. Albert was known as the seafaring prince because of his many ocean voyages and his keen interest

in marine biology. He founded the world-famous Oceanographic Museum in Monaco (and another in Paris). He also allowed for the creation of Monaco's first constitution in 1911, creating a limited democracy.

The Grimaldi royal family has lived in the palace for generations.

In the 20th century, the rule of Prince Louis II was a less happy time. His pro-Nazi sympathies and policies divided the people and infuriated his grandson, Rainier. Prince Rainier III took the throne in 1949 and ruled for 56 years, the longest reign of any European prince.

This statue of Prince Albert I stands in the Saint Martin Gardens of Monaco.

CONSTITUTIONAL MONARCHY

The Grimaldis had no real check on their authority until 1911, when Prince Albert I agreed to Monaco's first constitution after mass protests by citizens. The people—adult male citizens at least—were given a limited voice in the government through an elected National Council. The council could pass new laws, which then had to be approved by the prince. However, in 1959, after a dispute with the council, Prince Rainier III suspended parts of the constitution,

THE REVOLUTION OF 1910

Prince Albert I did not just give Monaco's citizens a constitution out of the goodness of his heart. Rather, they demanded one through a mostly peaceful revolution, a series of protests in 1910. They threatened to overthrow the monarchy and start a republic if their demands were not heard—and in January 1911, the new constitution was established. The prince, perhaps saving face, declared it "a gift" to his subjects. Even after this, protests continued for a while, with citizens demanding that more ties with France be cut and that a national treasury be established. At one point, protesters stormed the palace and looted it, although the prince escaped safely. On March 29, 1910, the New York Times *called it "a revolution in a teacup."*

dissolved the National Council, and, in 1961, created a National Assembly made up of people whom he had appointed.

The crisis with France over the taxation issue forced Prince Rainier III to reconsider his actions. To satisfy French president de Gaulle as well as his own people, Prince Rainier III got rid of his National Assembly, restored the National Council, and granted a more liberal constitution in 1962.

The National Council originally consisted of 18 members, but this number has since been changed to 24. Sixteen members are elected by majority vote, and eight others are elected on the basis of proportional representation—a formula based on the percentage of votes that each party received in the last election. Voting is by universal suffrage, and the members' terms are for five years.

In the early 21st century, a few main political parties were formed in Monaco. There has been some change since then, but by the 2018 elections, the main parties included the Union Monegasque, Horizon Monaco, and the new Primo! Priorité Monaco. In the most recent elections, which took place in February 2018, the Primo! Priorité Monaco party won 21 seats on the council. Horizon Monaco took two seats, and Union Monegasque took one. The next elections will take place in 2023.

The council shares legislative power with the prince, who has the power to initiate laws that the council then votes on. Only the monarch can ratify

laws once passed. The day-to-day functions of government are conducted by the minister of state. In the past, the minister had to be a French citizen. They were appointed by the prince from a list provided by the French government. That requirement, which gave France considerable influence over Monaco's government, has since been changed. The minister can now be a citizen of Monaco. They are also assisted by five other ministers, heading up departments of the interior; finance and economy; health and social affairs; public works, the environment, and urban development; and foreign affairs and cooperation.

The judiciary system has been modeled on that of France since 1819. Trials are held before a panel of three judges, rather than a single judge and a jury. Two French judges form a Court of Appeals.

The prince is also advised by two committees, the Crown Council and State Council. The seven members of the Crown Council advise on matters of the constitution and the state, and the 12 members of the State Council advise on matters of legislation. Neither group has any decision-making powers.

INTERNET LINKS

monacodc.org/institutions.html
This website of the Embassy of Monaco in Washington, D.C., talks about the governmental institutions of Monaco.

www.monaco-tribune.com/en/house-of-grimaldi/
This page tracks more than 700 years of the Grimaldi family in Monaco.

www.chicagotribune.com/sns-rainier-story.html
This is the 2005 *Chicago Tribune* obituary for Prince Rainier III.

ECONOMY

Today, the population of Monaco tends to be quite
wealthy. Fancy sports cars and designer fashion abound.

4

TODAY, THE MENTION OF MONACO immediately brings up images of fancy sports cars, glittering casinos, luxurious resorts, and designer fashion— and really, pretty much everything associated with wealth. However, things were not always this way.

In the 1860s, tiny Monaco was not the wealthy land it is now. In fact, it was in a good deal of financial trouble. When the regions of Menton and Roquebrune declared their independence in 1848, they reduced Monaco's land area by a huge amount and left Monaco with little arable land. These provinces were major food producers for Monaco. In addition, the products of those provinces, especially oranges, lemons, and olive oil, were the major sources of revenue for the state.

The loss of revenue and the need to import food plunged Monaco into very hard times. Since those difficult years, however, a number of tactics and the creative planning of several monarchs have not only restored the economy of the principality but have also given it one of the world's highest standards of living.

TAKING A CHANCE

While Prince Charles III gets much of the credit for bringing casino gambling to Monaco, the idea first belonged to his mother, Princess Caroline, wife of Prince Florestan. She had visited a spa in Hesse-Homburg, Germany, and recalled the casino there. She convinced her son that such a thing might help with Monaco's financial troubles.

The city-state of Monaco has monopolies in a few areas, including the telephone network and postal service. This means there is only one provider of these services.

At first, the casino project went in fits and starts. The first one opened in 1856. A number of different people ran it, with new ones taking over as the others failed. There were a number of temporary locations while new casinos were built in presumably better locations. Also, there were not many transportation options into Monaco, which limited the amount of people visiting. The venture was not exactly an instant success—far from it.

Finally, the casino landed in the area then called les Spelugues, or the Caves. Princess Caroline talked François Blanc, manager of the casino in Hesse-Homburg, into coming to Monaco to manage the facility in 1863. With the further addition of a railroad into Monaco, things started to turn around—so much so that Monaco did away with income taxes in 1869. Blanc renamed the casino area "Monte Carlo" in honor of Prince Charles III. He also started redesigning and expanding the casino.

The Casino de Monte-Carlo was constructed in three stages. First was the Salon de l'Europe, with eight magnificent crystal chandeliers later added in 1898. For the second phase, the prince hired Europe's leading architect, Charles Garnier, who had just completed the great Paris Opera. Garnier created an extravagant building with frescoes. The Salle Garnier was completed in 1878, the same year as the great entrance hall with its 28 marble columns. The third part, the Salle Médecin, was completed in 1910.

The opulent surroundings proved to be a great attraction in their own right, especially for the wealthiest people of Europe and America. Prince Charles III also added other luxury elements: Les Thermes Marins de Monte-Carlo, for example, is a fantastic spa, featuring special treatments such as shiatsu massages, a pool of heated seawater, and a skin treatment with diamond dust. In addition, Monte Carlo offers some of Europe's most extravagant hotels and restaurants. The Hôtel de Paris includes a gold-decorated restaurant named Le Louis XV, which today boasts one of the world's largest wine cellars—about 350,000 bottles stored in a rock cave.

Ownership and management of the casino is in the hands of a corporation: the Société des Baines de Mer (Society of Sea Bathing; SBM). SBM continues to operate today, controlled by the government, and it is Monaco's main employer.

The corporation also owns and operates several of the most luxurious hotels and restaurants.

The combination of excellent facilities, a sun-filled Mediterranean climate, the beach and harbor facilities, and the lure of gambling provided Monaco with enormous potential as a year-round resort destination, and its success surpassed the most optimistic dreams. By the 1880s and 1890s, Monte Carlo was the jewel of European resort areas, drawing the wealthiest and most famous families from throughout Europe and the Americas.

The heyday of the Monte Carlo complex continued through the 1920s. The Roaring Twenties brought new visitors and spenders. Famous movie stars, great sports figures, jazz musicians, and even American underworld figures

The Casino de Monte-Carlo attracts people from around the world. The Salon de l'Europe is shown here.

were attracted to Monte Carlo. All they had to do was follow Monte Carlo's rules of dress and conduct in order to enter the casino and the best hotels and restaurants. In 1929, the first Formula One Grand Prix automobile race—a prestigious event that continues to be a major attraction—took place. Wealthy spectators watch the event and the preliminary races from the hotel terraces or from yachts in the harbor, while the Grimaldis enjoy the spectacle from their royal box.

Income generated by the casino, hotels, and restaurants suffered during the Great Depression of the 1930s. The legalization of some forms of gambling in parts of France also cut into Monte Carlo's revenues. However, Monte Carlo recovered from the hard times and continues to be the showcase of the principality—and the entire Mediterranean coast. Gambling operations still provide an important source of income, but they now constitute a lesser percentage of Monaco's revenue.

MORE THAN THE CASINO

When Prince Rainier III ascended the throne in 1949, he was determined to diversify the economy. He knew that income from the casino alone would not allow for the kind of growth he had in mind for Monaco. During his 56-year reign, Rainier used creative approaches to expand the economy and find new sources of revenue. The prince was remarkably successful and, by 2000, the casino's revenues amounted to only about 5 percent of the principality's income, a statistic that stands at about 4 percent today. Each of the following economic sectors now make important contributions to the economy.

NEW LAND, NEW INDUSTRIES Between 1966 and 1973, one of Prince Rainier's major projects was using landfill to create a sizeable expansion of Monaco's area through land reclamation. The new land became the principality's industrial area. Foreign corporations have been invited to build small, nonpolluting industrial facilities. These include cosmetic, pharmaceutical, plastic, and precision medical equipment companies. The companies provide jobs for local residents as well as tax revenues for the government.

This is not the only land reclamation project. The size of Port Hercules was extended to allow for bigger ships and a yacht club. And now, the Portier Cove project (expected to be finished by 2025) will add 15 more acres (6 ha) to the country. It is expected to hold apartments, villas, business, and a new marina.

TOURISM   From the beginning of his rule, Prince Rainier sought ways to expand Monaco's tourism. By combining improved beach facilities with advertising campaigns all over the world, the principality now draws vacationers throughout the year. The prince's plan to have a floating dock built in Spain and towed into the harbor has doubled the port's capacity. The harbor is constantly filled with yachts and sailboats, and the berths for cruise ships are considered some of the finest in the world.

Hotels, restaurants, and shops, as well as beach and harbor facilities, all provide jobs for residents. Jobs include standard hotel and restaurant positions,

Millions of tourists visit Monaco every year. This trackless tourist train provides another way for them to get around.

managerial posts, and many support services, such as delivery, food supplies, and limousine services. Tourism now draws an estimated 7 million visitors a year, with proceeds accounting for about 11 percent of the economy.

OTHER SOURCES OF REVENUE   Monaco's refusal to have an income tax caused considerable friction with France in the years after World War II. Wealthy French people and businesses were moving to Monaco in order to avoid France's income tax. Prince Rainier III finally relented and reached an agreement with the French government in the 1960s. French citizens who became residents after January 1957 must pay French income tax. Monegasque companies that do more than 25 percent of their business outside of Monaco also must pay taxes. These taxes provide one of the government's sources of income. In total, tax money now represents about 45 percent of Monaco's revenue.

Monaco receives income from several other sources, including the telephone network and the postal service. It also has a monopoly on tobacco. Slightly

Banking is an important business in Monaco. This photo shows the Barclays bank building in Monte Carlo on a sunny summer day.

REAL ESTATE

Unsurprisingly, real estate in Monaco is pricey—very pricey. Because of the small size of the city-state and the density of the population, demand is high, but supply is low. The average home costs about $4,500 per square foot, with more sought-after property about double that. Even a small apartment costs about $1.6 million to buy, and prices jumped more than 18 percent from 2017 to 2019 (although they hit a small decline then). It is the most expensive luxury residential market in the world, ahead of Hong Kong and New York City—where even luxury properties only cost about half as much. The next few years are expected to be a little more stable on the property front, however, as the uncertainly of the COVID-19 pandemic affects prices.

more than half the annual revenue comes from taxes on hotels, restaurant meals, banks, and industries. Monaco's postage stamps have been popular for years with collectors and tourists; the state holds a monopoly on their manufacture and sale.

Another important source of income—and employment—is provided by foreign companies that have established offices in Monaco to take advantage of the principality's low tax rates. To service these companies, the city-state provides banking and other financial services. These services, of course, are also available to Monaco's wealthy citizens. The principality also operates its own radio and television networks, although the television transmitter had to be situated on Mount Agel in France to achieve the necessary height.

INTO THE FUTURE

With its varied sources of income, Monaco has become prosperous. The people enjoy one of the highest standards of living in the world, with a gross national income of about $173,000 (145,000 euros) for residents. Almost one in every three people living there is a millionaire, and there is no poverty. (At least, there is no reported poverty. With no income tax, Monaco does not keep figures on such things, but the average income, employment, and real estate prices make poverty unlikely.)

This 2020 photo shows construction on a new area of Monaco, reclaimed from the sea.

Monaco continues to look for ways to improve and expand the economy. The Portier Cove project is in progress. The city-state is seeing growth in professional firms, shipping businesses, and technology. However, the COVID-19 pandemic that spread in 2020 took a toll on the country, as it did everywhere in the world. COVID-19 reached Monaco in February 2020, and Prince Albert II was the first head of state in the world to test positive for it in March 2020, though he recovered. The Monaco Grand Prix was canceled for the first time since 1929, and various other events and tourist attractions were temporarily stopped or closed.

Health organization recommendations that people not travel during the pandemic kept people from visiting Monaco, a hit to the tourism industry.

By early 2021, most museums, casinos, and other venues were open in the city-state, but it is still too soon to tell what sort of impact the long-reaching effects of the pandemic will have on Monaco. Because of its reliance on tourism and banking, economic downturns in other countries can have big effects on its own economy.

INTERNET LINKS

www.hellomonaco.com/sightseeing/monte-carlo-casino/unknown-facts-about-monaco-casino-de-monte-carlo/
This article includes photos and facts about the history of the Monte Carlo Casino.

money.cnn.com/2015/05/29/luxury/monaco-rich-millionaire-tax/index.html
CNN Business examines the wealth of the Monaco city-state.

www.reuters.com/article/us-monaco-extension/crowded-monaco-reclaims-land-to-build-more-luxury-flats-with-sea-view-idUSKBN1ZE1Y4
This 2020 article by news service Reuters details the Portier Cove project.

ENVIRONMENT

Colored recycling bins in Monaco are shown here. The city-state has developed a reputation for being environmentally conscious.

MONACO HAS A HISTORY OF BEING environmentally responsible, which may have started with Prince Albert I back in the late 19th century. Before and during his reign from 1889 to 1922, he studied oceanography, the science of the oceans, and was fascinated with the polar regions of Earth. This helped him gain an interest in protecting the environment. In 1921, long before the modern environmental movement began, he spoke to members of the U.S. National Academy of Sciences, warning of changes in and pressures on the seabed.

His namesake great-great-grandson has continued an interest in such things. When Prince Albert II succeeded his father Rainier in 2005, one of his first acts was to sign the Kyoto Protocol. Each nation that signs the protocol agrees to reduce the amount of greenhouse emissions in their nation as a way of protecting the world's ozone layer. Only a handful of countries, including the United States, have refused to ratify the protocol, arguing that reducing emissions will harm the economy and result in a loss of jobs.

5

Monaco's citizens are encouraged to use public transportation to reduce the amount of vehicle emissions.

In signing the Kyoto Protocol, Prince Albert II was going on record saying that tiny Monaco would be a model in the worldwide struggle to reverse the destruction of the planet's air, water, land, and quality of life. This was only the beginning in Monaco's efforts to become more environmentally aware and responsible. The city-state has made it a point to recruit nonpolluting businesses, for the sake of its residents and tourists as well as the world at large.

AN INFORMATIVE TRIP

On April 16, 2006, newspapers around the world printed variations on this news headline: "Monaco's Ruler Reaches North Pole." At least one subhead read: "Monaco's Prince Albert has reached the North Pole on his four-day expedition to highlight global warming."

The trip was carefully orchestrated, and the prince held several news conferences in the month prior to the actual journey to the pole. He knew that

Prince Albert II looks around the VENTURI Antarctica, the first electric polar exploration vehicle, in 2018. The prince has visited both Antarctica and the Arctic region.

the idea of the ruler of a Mediterranean resort principality traveling to the Arctic cold would draw the attention of journalists. In a press conference, he explained, "If in our modest way, by this action we are able to bring environmental problems to the forefront and force some leaders to take stronger actions, this expedition will have achieved its objectives."

Prince Albert II's great-great-grandfather, Prince Albert I, had made four Arctic trips in the early 1900s, but the current prince's venture was the first North Pole journey by any head of state while in office. On the last leg of the journey, Prince Albert II left the expedition's base camp in Russia on April 12, 2006, for the four-day dash to the North Pole. He led a team of seven, traveling by dogsled. The prince said it was a "physically difficult" journey. Two members of the team fell into the icy waters, but both were uninjured. The prince planted the flag of Monaco, as well as the flag of the International Olympic Committee, of which he is a member, at the North Pole.

On the day of his return to his camp, Prince Albert II used the publicity to hammer home his message. He talked about seeing evidence of global warming, such as shrinking glaciers. "We must try to find solutions [to global warming]," he said at a press conference, "with scientists, obviously, but also at the individual level … I think everyone, by their behavior can make small contributions to a global and extraordinary effort."

In 2009, the prince also traveled across Antarctica, visiting scientific bases and learning about the region and the problems facing it.

FOUNDATIONS AND PROGRAMS

The same year he visited the North Pole, Prince Albert II started a foundation bearing his name dedicated to donating money to environmental projects, including those to limit climate change, to encourage renewable energy sources, to protect biodiversity, and to manage water resources and fight desertification. It focuses on the Mediterranean basin, the polar regions, and the less-developed countries of the world, and since it started, it has donated more than $68 million (57 million euros) to more than 530 environmental projects.

Monaco has other programs dedicated to the environment as well. The government launched a "Responsible Trading" program in 2014, promoting and supporting environmentally responsible practices. In 2017, a Responsible Trading label was introduced, meant to identify traders that had responsible and eco-friendly business practices, including reducing waste and moving away from single-use items. There is also a Responsible Restaurant label.

The prince was also one of the founders of the CleanEquity conference in 2008. The conference encourages sustainability in businesses by inviting selected business owners to visit for the event and giving them the chance to get financing, promote their business, and find new business partners.

UNIQUE ISSUES

In many ways, Monaco is a small city, although it is also a sovereign state with the same rights and responsibilities as nations that are hundreds of times larger. Since it has no polluting industries and no runoff from agricultural

Jessica Sbaraglia, founder of Terre de Monaco, shows off fresh produce grown in a rooftop garden.

lands, the principality has avoided many of the environmental problems faced by most larger countries. However, Monaco does face several familiar environmental issues.

One problem is urban crowding. Monaco is one of the world's most densely populated nations. Practically all other countries appear less crowded because forests, farm regions, and other open areas change the statistics. Issues such as vehicular emissions, sewage, and garbage removal are causes for concern. The principality has made agreements with French companies to provide sewage treatment and landfills for garbage. There are also strict rules for recycling, and recycled materials are also sent to France.

The many gardens of Monaco, including this Japanese garden, are watered with reclaimed water.

While an extensive (and expensive) new development might not seem to be the most environmentally friendly thing, the Portier Cove project in Monaco is aiming to be just that. The new area will have a 15-acre (6 ha) eco-friendly district, which is being built to strict environmental standards meant to conserve the ocean area. Protected plant species were carefully transferred before building started, and measures were taken to protect other sea life. Much of the energy used in building this project is from renewable sources. Even its shape is meant to conform to the coastline so important ocean currents are not affected. Also, once built, the new district will be meant for pedestrians and bicyclists.

Because Monaco is so small, water conservation and sanitation are very important. The government has taken steps to make this a priority. The city-state's extensive number of parks and gardens are managed by conserving water and limiting the use of chemicals. Urban farming is beginning to take hold as well. Businesses plant vegetable farms on rooftops and terraces, providing fresh produce to hotels and restaurants.

PROTECTING THE SEA

Monaco occupies a relatively small space between the Mediterranean Sea and the mountains. This has made the people and the government keenly aware of how changes in the world's oceans can affect their city-state. In trying to alert world leaders to the dangers of global warming, Prince Albert II pointed out that as the world's ice caps continue to melt at an unprecedented rate, the melting ice will cause a rise in ocean levels that may be disastrous to coastal cities throughout the world.

All of Monaco's territorial waters are part of the Pelagos Marine Sanctuary. Two marine reserves also exist to protect native species. In addition, Prince Albert II's foundation founded a rescue center for marine species in 2019.

Monaco's Oceanographic Museum has been playing an important role in matters relating to the Mediterranean Sea and the world's oceans. The museum was built in the early 1900s by Prince Albert I. It is a large and impressive

structure built against the face of a 250-foot (76 m) cliff. The museum's aquarium has living displays of many Mediterranean and tropical species.

The famous oceanographer and cinematographer Jacques-Yves Cousteau directed the museum for around 30 years, and his films are still shown in the lecture hall. Below the aquarium are the research laboratories that were used by Cousteau and a revolving team of scientists. In 1984, it was in the laboratories that Cousteau's scientists identified fast-growing algae, nicknamed the "killer algae" because it blocks the sunlight from reaching native plants. Although the discovery of the bright-green algae seemed timely, the algae was already spreading at a fantastic rate. The killer algae originated in the

Monaco's Oceanographic Museum (Musée Océanographique) draws many visitors each year.

While Monaco has little wildlife, gardens such as the Jardin Exotique, part of which is shown here, help give the city-state its own touch of green.

Pacific Ocean and has now covered a huge area along the Mediterranean coast. The museum's scientists are working with specialists from several countries to reverse the spread of the algae without harming other plant life.

As more people become interested in ecotourism and traveling in an environmentally friendly way, Monaco's focus on protecting its environment could be a boon to its economy as well. The tourism sector of the region is part of the sustainability measures, tapping into the rise of sustainable and responsible tourism. In 2018, the Monaco Government & Tourist Convention

Authority started a "Green Is the New Glam" campaign, bringing attention to Monaco's efforts toward sustainability and trying to attract tourists who are looking for a progressive and environmentally friendly destination. Even the public transportation system runs on electricity or biofuels, and the city-state hopes to be carbon neutral by 2050.

Noise pollution is carefully monitored in Monaco as well, protecting the region's sea creatures and other wildlife.

INTERNET LINKS

www.bbc.com/travel/story/20200114-the-glitzy-european-city-going-green
An article from the BBC discusses how Monaco is going green.

www.euro.who.int/en/health-topics/environment-and-health/Climate-change/country-work/monacos-sustainable-resilience-approach-to-climate-change
The World Health Organization Office for Europe reports on Monaco's approach to climate change.

www.latimes.com/environment/story/2020-02-13/an-interview-with-prince-albert-ii-of-monaco-on-the-state-of-the-planet
This 2020 *Los Angeles Times* interview with Prince Albert II highlights efforts to protect the environment.

news.bbc.co.uk/2/hi/europe/4914898.stm
This article reports on Prince Albert II's trip to the North Pole.

MONEGASQUES

Monaco has a unique sort of population, with the native people a minority in their own country.

W HILE MONACO HAS ABOUT 38,000 people, most of these people are originally from other countries. In fact, nearly 70 percent of the city-state's population is from other nations—about 125 of them. The largest demographic (25 percent) is from France, followed by Italy (19 percent), both of which are its closest neighbors. About 300 U.S. citizens (1 percent) live there as well.

Monaco's native people, Monegasques, make up only about 22.5 percent of the population, a little more than one-fifth of Monaco's people. One is considered Monegasque through bloodline: They are born to a Monegasque parent. Someone who marries a Monegasque person may also be eligible for citizenship after at least 10 years have passed. There are also cases in which the prince of Monaco bestows citizenship.

Les enfants du pays ("the children of the country") are residents who have lived in the country for a number of years but are not eligible for citizenship. There are a few ways to be considered a resident of Monaco, including through employment, business, or wealth, all with very specific rules.

As far as root ethnicity goes for Monagasques, the national and ethnic makeup of the population reflects a history of people moving into the area over many centuries.

6

At one time, someone could claim citizenship in Monaco after their family had lived there for three generations, but that is no longer the case.

A LAND OF MANY POPULATIONS

Monaco, including the French coastal regions to the east (Menton and Roquebrune), has been home to a wide variety of people. Settlers from ancient Greece moved in around 600 BCE, establishing a trading colony named Monoikos. Around 125 BCE, the Romans began a gradual takeover of the entire Mediterranean coastal region. They made Monoikos into Rome's first *provincia* (province) beyond the Alps, which gave the name "Provence" to this area of southern France. Some of the earliest architecture in greater Monaco dates from the Roman period, including the foundations of fortresses and the remains of amphitheaters and roads.

Following the collapse of the Roman Empire, various Germanic tribes, including the Visigoths and Ostrogoths, invaded the area, destroying many towns and Roman buildings. Some of the invaders who originally came from eastern Europe and western Asia remained and intermarried with the local populations.

Around 1000 CE, Italian city-states took control of much of the Mediterranean coast. While the Guelf and Ghibelline parties vied for control of the Monaco area, families from Genoa moved in. Some remained in separate Genoese enclaves, while others mixed with the Monegasque population. Many Monegasques today continue to speak a dialect that is based on Genoese Italian. The Grimaldi family, one of the powerful clans of Genoa, became the ruling family of Monaco.

The Grimaldi realm included Menton and Roquebrune as well as what is now considered Monaco. This realm was prosperous from the 14th century through the late 18th century. The government relied on revenue obtained from taxing the area's lemons, oranges, and olive oil. As the taxes became an increasingly heavy burden, the people of Menton and Roquebrune began to rebel, some wanting independence and others preferring to be annexed by France.

Monaco is not all glitz and glamour. There is a lot of history down some of those narrow streets.

Following the French Revolution, which began in 1789, the revolutionary French government captured Monaco and imprisoned the Grimaldi royal family. Monegasques hated French rule, which closed churches and turned them into "Temples of Reason." In 1815, after the fall of Napoleon, the Grimaldis once again ruled greater Monaco, although the region was placed under the protection of the king of Sardinia. Even today, Monegasques do not at all consider themselves part of France. They have their own distinct history and culture.

Monegasques have access to housing options that allow them to stay in their country.

MONEGASQUES THROUGH THE YEARS

The population of Monaco changed dramatically from the mid-1800s through the 1900s. First, Monaco lost about 90 percent of its territory when Menton and Roquebrune pulled away in 1848 and the Grimaldis recognized the area as part of France in 1861. The loss of this area removed the Grimaldis' major source of revenue and also a sizeable portion of Monaco's population, including people of both Italian and French descent.

The makeup of the population of Monaco proper also began to change. One major change came from the emergence of Monaco and the Mediterranean coast as a great resort area. A new trend may have been started by Tobias Smollett, a famous Scottish physician and novelist. On a visit to the coast about 6 miles (9.7 km) west of Monaco in 1763 or 1764, Smollett took the extraordinary action of bathing in the Mediterranean Sea, part of his search for a cure to a lung illness. He then wrote about his experience and urged others to follow his lead.

The idea of sea-bathing and vacationing on the coast was given an additional push by another famous Englishman, Henry Lord Brougham. He built a large villa in Cannes, France, in 1834 and publicized the area as ideal for health and vacationing. Over the next 50 years, no fewer than 50 hotels were built, catering to wealthy Europeans.

Also in the mid-1800s, a guidebook named the entire coastal area the Côte d'Azur (Azure Coast). The name stuck; it seemed to be a perfect label for the deep blue of the usually cloudless sky. The same region was also called the French Riviera, and both names added luster to the coast and served to attract more and more people. By the 1890s, a vacation on the Côte d'Azur became the

While many famous people live in Monaco, most of them are from other countries. A number of racing drivers, perhaps unsurprising due to Monaco's history with the Grand Prix, are Monegasques, including Louis Chiron, Olivier Beretta, Charles Leclerc, and Arthur Leclerc. Otherwise, the most famous Monegasques tend to be members of the royal family. When Prince Rainier III married Grace Kelly, he brought the family even more into the world spotlight. Prince Albert II and his sisters, Princesses Caroline and Stéphanie, have been in that spotlight their entire lives—as have their children and, in some cases, their grandchildren.

favored destination for wealthy Europeans. When England's famous monarch Queen Victoria began to spend winters near Nice, France, in the 1880s, the advertising picture was complete.

As more and more people flocked to the Côte d'Azur, or French Riviera, including Monaco, they added new elements to the population. The opening of Monaco's Monte Carlo Casino in 1863 encouraged some wealthy people to settle in Monaco, adding English, Germans, Italians, and Russians to the principality's population. A few wealthy Americans also discovered Monaco, including railroad tycoons such as the Vanderbilts and the Goulds.

Artists were also drawn to Monaco and the surrounding area by the intensity and clarity of the light and the picturesque views of countless villages. Matisse, Renoir, and other great Impressionists settled in the area, some permanently. Later, renowned artists such as Pablo Picasso and Jean Cocteau designed sets for Les Ballets de Monte-Carlo.

In the 20th century, some of the Americans who settled in Monaco were drawn by literary figures who lived there, at least on a part-time basis. F. Scott Fitzgerald and H. G. Wells were among the writers who helped make Monaco a popular place to live. Sports figures and entertainers have also moved there part-time, adding to the allure. Actor Leonardo DiCaprio and singer-philanthropist Bono are among other celebrities who have bought homes just outside Monaco, as did earlier movie stars such as John Wayne and Humphrey Bogart.

Many of the wealthy and famous people who have moved to Monaco have taken up permanent residency, some because of the loose tax laws. They are part of a varied population that is unlike that of any other country.

In part because of the small size of the Monegasque population, the people tend to have a close relationship to the royal family and each other. The palace courtyard is opened for special events such as royal weddings and births, and all Monegasque children are invited to the children's Christmas party that takes place there every year.

Monegasques wave the flag of Monaco during National Day in November.

INTERNET LINKS

www.euronews.com/travel/2014/10/13/not-all-the-monegasques-are-billionnaires
This Euro News article discusses the local Monegasque population in Monaco.

www.monaco-tribune.com/en/2019/10/monegasque-nationality-imposed-marriage-duration-could-rise-to-20-years/
This article looks at how the number of years of marriage before the spouse of a native Monegasque person can claim citizenship might soon increase and why.

www.monaco-tribune.com/en/2020/04/lockdown-and-daily-life-how-have-monegasques-coped/
A local news article examines how Monegasques dealt with the COVID-19 pandemic in 2020.

LIFESTYLE

Monaco is small enough that it is easy to walk to get where you need to go—although the streets can be quite steep at times.

LIFE IN MONACO IS BOTH JUST LIKE
and totally unlike anywhere else. On
one hand, typical Monegasque families
go to work and school and take part in
leisure activities just like anyone else. On
the other hand, much of the atmosphere of
their city-state is unusual. There is a huge
percentage of millionaires living there, no
poverty, and a baseline of relative luxury.
Most workers (about 80 percent, according
to a 2019 study) live outside Monaco
itself, in less expensive areas in France.
It's common to cross the borders between
the countries multiple times a day.

Many Monegasque families live much like modestly well-to-do families
in other cities of Europe or the United States. Those who were born in
Monaco, or who have lived there for at least five years, enjoy the city-
state's status as a tax haven. Depending on their income level, people
who do not have to pay income taxes can see their income rise by 40 to
50 percent.

Although there is no typical lifestyle in Monaco, the following two
sections will give you a glimpse of how two large segments of the
population live.

7

Monaco's etiquette
practices are much
like French etiquette
standards, with even
more of an emphasis
on privacy.

Densely packed apartment buildings rise over Port Hercules in Monaco.

EVERYDAY PEOPLE

An average middle-income family might consist of two parents and two children. Many of these middle-income families take up residence in high-rise apartments that sometimes overlook Monaco's harbor. This part of the city feels crowded, with large apartment buildings standing shoulder-to-shoulder on the steep hillside. From the harbor, the city presents a wall of high-rises. Many adult Monegasques work in managerial positions for manufacturing companies or in the service industry, supporting Monaco's main tourism industry. Children attend schools locally or boarding schools abroad.

Middle-income parents take turns preparing meals, and the family might eat together on their apartment's balcony, with a view of the yacht-filled harbor and white sails beyond. Breakfast would typically consist of fruit or juice, a roll or croissant, and coffee or café au lait—much like in nearby France. Working adults often have their midday meal at a restaurant, while schoolchildren eat in school. The family usually eats dinner at home. Dinner is often a light affair comprising fresh greens, cheese, sausages, French bread, and sometimes wine. Parents often purchase supplies at covered marketplaces jammed with colorful stalls of flowers, herbs, fruits, and vegetables. These marketplaces are often open seven days a week all year. There is a lot of access to fresh produce and seafood.

Monegasques might take their visiting tourist friends to lunch at famous restaurants surrounded by lush gardens. They are well-known for "people watching," as passengers from cruise ships stroll past to go shopping. Monegasques and tourists both may shop in the neighborhood called the Golden Square, where exclusive shops feature clothing, jewelry, and cosmetics from every famous designer in Paris, Rome, London, and New York. However, there are less expensive areas, such as Les Révoires.

Monaco is so close (and easily accessible) to France that even the street signs point out locations in the other country.

Divorce rates are low in Monaco—about 4.8 per 1,000 marriages. However, more people today are living together rather than getting married.

For some light exercise, Monegasques may spend an hour walking through the Jardins du Casino, the luxurious green area surrounding the famous casino. Some people extend their encounter with nature by hiking along the coastal road that extends from Monte Carlo east to Roquebrune and beyond.

THE ULTRAWEALTHY

The lure of the Monte Carlo Casino in the mid-1800s, along with Monaco's lavish hotels and restaurants, brought hundreds of the wealthiest Europeans to the principality. This glittering era became known as the Belle Époque (the beautiful age). It continued into the early 20th century, with an influx of Hollywood stars and sports figures. The lifestyle of the rich and famous continues in Monaco today.

Many wealthy Monegasques or residents own yachts, and many of these are extravagant enough to have their own helicopter pads. Homes for the

A rooftop garden and pool sit atop an apartment building in Monaco.

wealthy are also luxurious, ranging from multimillion-dollar apartments to villas with a dozen bedrooms. Most of these homes have staffs of maids, cooks, gardeners, and servants. Some wealthy people are opera stars and singers; sports figures, including Grand Prix race drivers; and stars of films and television. Others are bankers or investors and retired owners of businesses.

Most of Monaco's wealthy have servants to take care of many of their needs, but many also devote some of their time and money to causes such as environmental protection, wildlife preservation, and a variety of charities. One of the most important annual events, for example, is the Red Cross Gala Ball, held in early August. Prince Albert II, along with his sisters, Princesses Stéphanie and Caroline, welcome guests to the Salle des étoiles of the Sporting d'Eté club. This is one of Europe's largest charity events, with more than 1,000 guests paying more than $1,000 each to attend.

PLAYGROUNDS FOR THE RICH

While many Monegasques are not as wealthy as the richest foreign nationals living in Monaco, they still have access to many of their playgrounds—with the notable exception of the casinos themselves, which aren't open to natives of Monaco— such as the many luxurious gardens, restaurants, clubs, hotels, and shops, including the streets of luxury boutiques (including such brands as Chanel and Cartier) and dozens of businesses in the upscale Metropole Shopping Center.

Another event designed for those with luxurious lifestyles is the annual Monaco Yacht Show, held in September. Hundreds of companies display yachting merchandise to more than 15,000 people. Visitors can board yachts and view hundreds of expensive accessories.

PRACTICAL CONCERNS

In Monaco, education is free and compulsory for children ages 6 to 16. Literacy rates are high, nearly 100 percent. There are seven nursery and primary schools, a secondary school for those 11 to 15, and a lycée (a secondary school that prepares students for college) for those ages 15 to 18. There are also a few private schools. Thousands of students are served by these schools.

There are some specialized schools in Monaco. The Technical Lycée of Monte Carlo offers training in hotel and restaurant management, as well as technical and commercial courses such as accounting, banking, and computer programming. Other specialized schools include the Princess Grace Academy of Classical Dance and the Rainier III Academy of Music.

Health standards are high, and Monegasques have access to a public health-care system with most of their costs reimbursed. That is reflected in the statistics for life expectancy in Monaco. Life expectancy at birth is 85.6 years for men and 93.4 years for women. Most doctors receive their training in France or other European countries. There are several hospitals, including the Princess Grace Hospital Centre, a modern facility with advanced equipment and treatments.

This photo shows a primary school in La Condamine. Children must start attending school by age six.

LGBTQ+ RIGHTS

Monaco is neither among the best nor the worst countries when it comes to LGBTQ+ rights. Same-sex relationships are legal, but same-sex couples and their families do not have the same legal protections that other couples do. There are no laws allowing transgender people to change their legal gender. Monaco also does not have legalized same-sex marriage. However, as of June 2020, the city-state accepts legal contracts between couples living together, including same-sex couples, that grant some of the rights and benefits that married couples have. Still, in 2020, the International Lesbian, Gay, Bisexual, Trans, and Intersex Association of Europe (ILGA-Europe) has rated Monaco as 45th out of 49 countries in Europe when it comes to LGBTQ+ rights.

Monaco is also a very safe country. It has a 24-hour video surveillance system that monitors most areas. Traffic laws and other rules are strict. It also has one of the largest police forces per capita in the world, with about 1 police officer for every 100 residents, and the officers must undergo an intensive two-year training program.

INTERNET LINKS

www.businessinsider.com/monaco-wealth-poverty-life-photos-2019-11#monaco-a-tiny-sovereign-city-state-on-the-french-riviera-is-so-wealthy-that-it-doesnt-even-measure-poverty-rates-1
This article shows what it is like to visit Monaco and its wealthy environment.

monacolife.net/most-workers-in-monaco-live-in-france/
This page has information on a 2019 study on how many employees in Monaco do not live in the city-state.

rainbow-europe.org/#8649/0/0
You can find ILGA-Europe's report and information on Monaco's LGBTQ+ rights record here.

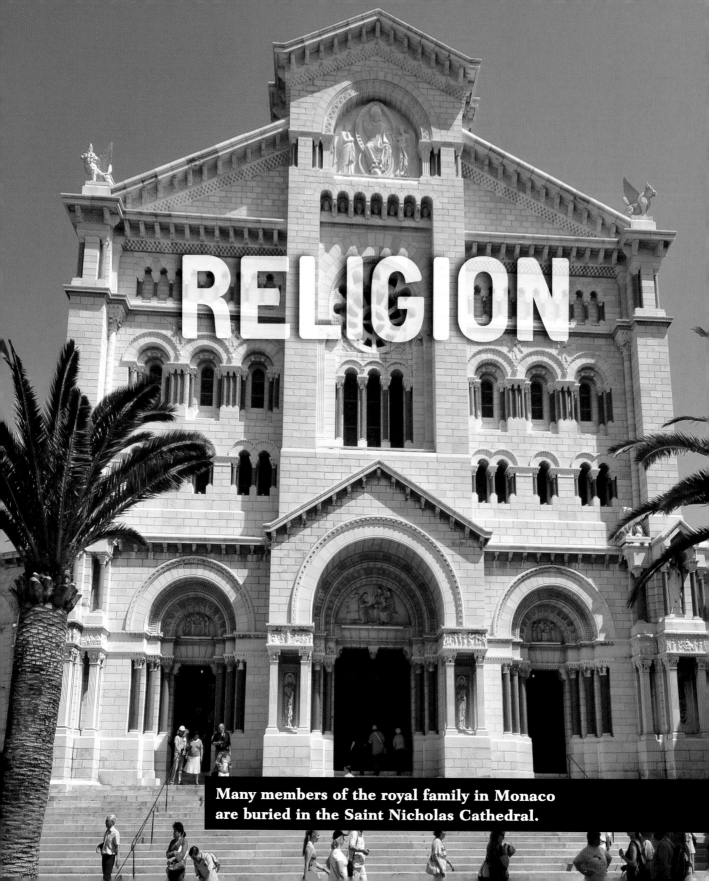

RELIGION

Many members of the royal family in Monaco are buried in the Saint Nicholas Cathedral.

T HE NATIVE PEOPLE OF MONACO ARE overwhelmingly Roman Catholic, probably unsurprising given that the very roots of the city-state involve the Guelfs, supporters of the Roman Catholic pope. This shows in festivals and observances throughout the region. The city-state makes up one archdiocese with six parishes, with one cathedral and five additional Catholic churches. Roman Catholicism is the official religion of Monaco, and more than 90 percent of the citizens consider themselves Catholic.

However, Monaco's constitution guarantees freedom of religion. No one is forced to take part in religious rituals or follow Catholicism, and according to reports from religious freedom organizations, other religions are socially accepted. There are few government restrictions as well, although groups must apply to the government for permission to build places of worship and be recognized.

Most Monegasques who do not identify as Roman Catholic still identify as Christian. Still, less than 5 percent of the population belongs to one of the Protestant Christian religions.

8

Monaco's grand cathedral is called the Cathedral of Our Lady Immaculate or Saint Nicholas Cathedral.

Monaco's Saint Nicholas Cathedral is an immense and historic building, one full of treasures and constructed on the Rock in Monaco's old town, on the site of an older church from the 14th century. It was built from 1875 to 1911, out of white stone from a nearby town in France, and it holds the tombs of many of the city-state's past rulers dating back to 1505. On the newer side of religious construction, Monaco's Synagogue Edmond Safra is only a handful of years old, constructed in Monte Carlo and finished in 2017. The large building is shaped like a Torah scroll.

CELEBRATION AND DEVOTION

There are Catholic religious festivals and holy days in almost every month of the year. January 26 and 27 mark the Feast of Saint Dévote, Monaco's patron saint.

In the spring, many Monegasques and other residents observe Lent, the 40 days leading up to Easter Sunday. During Lent, many people go to daily Mass services and take part in the Stations of the Cross—symbolically retracing the steps of Jesus Christ on the way to his crucifixion. The solemnity of Good Friday, with all church statues draped in mourning, is followed by the joyous music and prayers of Easter Sunday and Easter Monday.

On the days just before Ash Wednesday, which introduces the Lenten period of church services and partial fasting, the area explodes with a celebration called Carnival. For two days, people engage in a round of parties, parades, and feasts. The event is much like Carnival, or Mardi Gras, in other countries, including the U.S. city of New Orleans, Louisiana. The Carnival in Nice, France, less than 10 miles (16 km) from the Monaco border, is particularly well known.

Another popular religious festival celebrates Saint John's Day on June 24. On the eve of Saint John's Day, a crowd gathers on the Palace Square. Members of a Monegasque folk group—the Palladienne—wear historical costumes and sing and dance, accompanied by music played on mandolins. The costumes consist of long, frilly shirts and garments with red and white stripes. The Palladienne might be joined by folk groups from France, Italy, and Spain. Meanwhile, the

A religious icon is shown in Monaco's Saint Nicholas Cathedral.

royal family attends a service in the Palace Chapel, which is dedicated to Saint John the Baptist.

After the service, two footmen from the palace carry burning torches to the square, where they light a huge bonfire. On Saint John's Day itself, a procession forms in Monte Carlo. The folk groups create a guard around "Little Saint John" and his lamb and march through the streets. Music, dancing, and eating continue far into the night.

SAINT DÉVOTE

The roots of many religious practices go far back in time, some to the earliest days of Christianity, including the persecution of Christians in the third and fourth centuries by the Roman Empire. One of Monaco's favorite religious

Prince Albert II and Princess Charlene of Monaco take part in ceremonies for the Feast of Saint Dévote in 2015.

festivals—the Feast of Saint Dévote—dates from this era. Dévote is the patron saint of Monaco.

According to the legend, a young woman named Dévote, from the island of Corsica, was one of the victims of the Roman persecution in the early fourth century. Although she was tortured until she died, Dévote refused to renounce her faith. To deny her a Christian burial, the Romans planned to burn her body, but other Christians placed it in a small boat and set it adrift, hoping it would reach Africa, where she could be buried.

According to the story, a dove appeared (or flew out of the dead woman's mouth) and guided the leaking boat to a cove in Monaco. Dévote was buried on January 27. Many sailors and fishing families began praying at her grave site. Several miracles were attributed to her, and she was declared a saint by the Vatican.

Some years later, thieves stole Dévote's bones, planning to sell them as religious relics (objects with special religious or healing powers). Some sailors chased away the thieves, rescued the bones, and set the thieves' boat on fire.

The Feast of Saint Dévote on January 27 celebrates Dévote as the principality's patron saint. The royal family participates in the ceremonies, and the ruling prince puts a torch to a small boat, reenacting the burning of the thieves' boat. After a service in the chapel, during which the town and the harbor are blessed, the celebration includes the releasing of doves and a firework display in the harbor.

In the 11th century, a chapel was built on the spot where Dévote's boat allegedly landed.

MORE TRADITIONS

In addition to Dévote, Monegasques also celebrate another martyred figure—Saint Roman. According to the stories, Roman was a soldier in the army of the Roman Empire and was an early convert to Christianity. In the year 258, he was ordered to renounce his faith and, when he refused, he was executed. Like

Beautiful stained-glass windows decorate a church in Monaco.

Dévote, he became one of the Christian martyrs and was elevated to sainthood. His feast day, August 9, is celebrated with ancient hymns and a procession.

A number of holy days and festivals are spread throughout the year. Many are more typical of Roman Catholic observances, but some include local or regional traditions.

The Epiphany, for example, is celebrated on January 6, between New Year's Day and the Feast of Saint Dévote. People might buy a *galette des rois* (king's cake), a puff pastry with a creamy filling. The person who finds the *feve* (a bean) receives a crown and a reward. (The bean embedded in the cake is now usually a plastic or porcelain figurine.)

During the period before Easter, men in an organization called the Venerable Brotherhood of Black Penitents of Mercy hold special services. Dressed in black, they have a procession that reenacts the Stations of the Cross. The organization dates back to the Crusades, when Christians tried to capture the Holy Land. They conclude the ceremony with services at the Chapel of Mercy, built in the early 1600s.

Other traditional holy days include the Feast of the Ascension, on the 40th day after Easter, celebrating Jesus Christ's ascent into heaven. Pentecost, or Whitsunday, takes place on the seventh Sunday after Easter. It celebrates the descent of the Holy Spirit upon the disciples. On August 15, Catholics observe the Feast of the Assumption, celebrating the bodily taking of the Virgin Mary into heaven following her death.

Christmas celebrations vary, depending partly on where family traditions originated. Some Monegasques, for example, still follow an ancient tradition in which a young family member dips an olive branch into a glass of wine. The child then stands in front of the fireplace and makes the sign of the cross with the olive branch, while reciting a poem that glorifies the olive tree. Everyone then takes a sip of the wine before enjoying a meal of traditional Monegasque foods. One of those foods is usually *fougasse*—flat, crispy bread sprinkled with red and white aniseed.

OTHER RELIGIONS

Monaco has been home to a small number of Jews for many centuries. Before and during World War II (1939—1945), hundreds of Jewish refugees came from other parts of Europe, attempting to escape persecution by Nazi-controlled Germany. Some Monegasque officials tried to help Jews by providing fake documents, but Nazi agents discovered many of the refugees. The Nazis deported several hundred and sent them to concentration camps, where many died.

Somewhere between 1,000 and 2,000 Jews live in Monaco today, although most are not citizens. This adds up to at least 3 percent of the resident population, giving Monaco the highest percentage of Jewish residents anywhere outside of Israel. There is one synagogue in the city-state, built in 2017.

There are also a small number of Muslims in Monaco, most of them from North African countries. There are also frequent business visitors from the oil-producing states of the Persian Gulf, such as Kuwait and Saudi Arabia. There are no mosques, although the nearest is within walking distance over the border in France.

There are also very small numbers of people who follow other religions, including Hinduism and Buddhism, and a percentage who do not consider themselves religious at all.

INTERNET LINKS

www.state.gov/reports/2019-report-on-international-religious-freedom/monaco/
The website of the U.S. Department of State has a 2019 report on religious freedom in Monaco.

www.visitmonaco.com/us/place/monuments/94/cathedrale-de-monaco
The Visit Monaco website offers a look at the history of Monaco's cathedral.

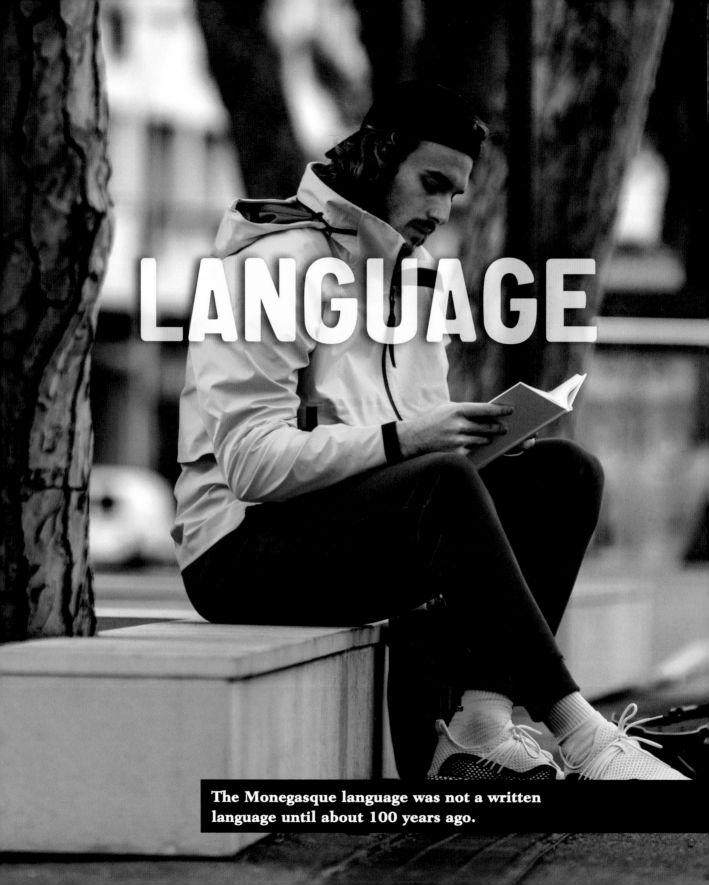

LANGUAGE

The Monegasque language was not a written language until about 100 years ago.

9

PEOPLE SPEAK MANY LANGUAGES IN Monaco, which is no surprise considering that people from more than 100 different nations live there. However, the official language is French, and more than half the residents of Monaco speak it. It is used in government documents, schools, media, and business. Many people also speak Italian and English.

There is also a local Monegasque language, a dialect of Ligurian. It is similar to Italian and, to some extent, French, with some things taken from the language of Genoa, dating back to the Middle Ages. About a fifth of the population—the native Monegasque people—speaks this language, which once nearly died out before having a renaissance of sorts.

SAVING MONEGASQUE

Monegasque was once only a spoken language. However, in the 1920s, some of Monaco's citizens started putting it down on paper and writing its rules of grammar. In 1927, *A Legenda de Santa Devota* by Louis Notari became the first work of literature in the Monegasque language. Since then, there have been short stories, theater works, poems, and more. Many books written in other languages have also been translated into Monegasque.

Prince Albert II of Monaco made a speech in the Monegasque language when he became ruling prince in 2005.

MONEGASQUE

Pàire nostru che sí ünt'u celu che u to nume sice santificàu che u to regnu arrive ünsci'a terra cuma ün celu sice fà a to' vuruntà. Dàne anchœi cuma tüt'i giurni u nostru pan. Perdùnane i nostri pecài cuma perdunamu a chëli che n'an fàu de mà. Nun ne làscia piyà da tentaçiun ma libérane d'u mà.

This sign outside a church in Monaco has the Pater Noster (Our Father), or Lord's Prayer, in the Monegasque language.

Despite all these efforts, the language was nearly extinct by the 1970s. Prince Rainier III started an initiative to save it, making classes on the language required in public schools and eventually private schools as well. Monegasque made a rebound after that. Today, some street signs in Monaco's old town feature the language along with French.

MORE ON FRENCH

In French, most letters are pronounced much like the letters in English. However, there are some special cases and a few general rules that are helpful.

Emphasize each syllable, but do not pronounce the last consonant of a word—including the plural *s*.

Hello . . . . Ciau
Good morning . . . . Bon giurnu *or* bungiurnu
Goodbye . . . . A se revede *or* ciau
Thanks so much . . . . . Merçí tantu
Yes . . . . Sci
No . . . . Nun
Pleased to meet you . . . . Uncantau
How much is this? . . . . . Qantu?
Please . . . . Per pieigé
Go Monaco! . . . . Daghe Mungu!

The letter *c* is pronounced like an English *k* when it comes before *a*, *o*, or *u*. Before *e* and *i*, it is pronounced like the *s* in "sun."

The letter *h* is always silent. The letter *j* is pronounced like the *s* in "leisure," and it is often written phonetically as *zh*. The letter *r* is pronounced from the back of the throat to roll it. (This comes with practice and listening.)

When a syllable ends in an *n* or *m*, these letters are not pronounced, but the vowel that comes before them is given a nasal pronunciation.

The pronouns *vous* and *tu* can be troublesome for visitors and newcomers. Both mean "you," but *tu* is a more intimate word. It is used to refer to someone you know very well or when speaking to children or animals. When addressing any adult who is not a close friend, one should always use *vous*. Trouble arises when visitors, in an effort to be friendly, use *tu* too readily, even with people they have just met.

NONVERBAL COMMUNICATION

Sometimes actions and even facial expressions can communicate just as much as spoken words. Anthropologist Edward T. Hall called this nonverbal communication "the silent language."

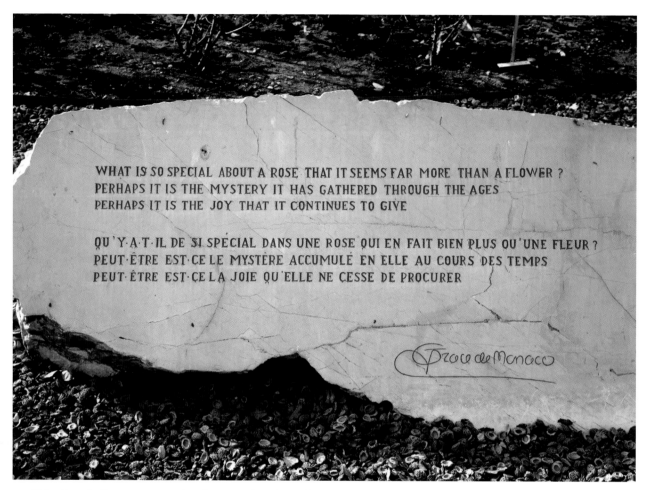

WHAT IS SO SPECIAL ABOUT A ROSE THAT IT SEEMS FAR MORE THAN A FLOWER ?
PERHAPS IT IS THE MYSTERY IT HAS GATHERED THROUGH THE AGES
PERHAPS IT IS THE JOY THAT IT CONTINUES TO GIVE

QU'Y·A·T·IL DE SI SPÉCIAL DANS UNE ROSE QUI EN FAIT BIEN PLUS QU'UNE FLEUR ?
PEUT·ÊTRE EST·CE LE MYSTÈRE ACCUMULÉ EN ELLE AU COURS DES TEMPS
PEUT·ÊTRE EST·CE LA JOIE QU'ELLE NE CESSE DE PROCURER

Grace de Monaco

This stone in the Princess Grace Rose Garden in Monaco has text in English and French.

Like the people of southern France, for example, Monegasques often gesture a good deal with their hands as they talk. Visitors sometimes get the impression that the person is very emotional or overly excited.

Similarly, when a man and woman or two women greet one another, they may kiss each other lightly on the cheek, usually once or twice. Men usually shake hands.

Choosing the wrong word is another way in which misunderstandings can occur. When introducing a Monegasque person to another person, saying only the person's name may seem overly familiar. To be on the safe side, some travel consultants say, it is always best to introduce the person as "Madame," "Monsieur," or "Mademoiselle," followed by their name.

SOME WORDS AND PHRASES IN FRENCH

Hello	Bonjour
Goodbye	Au revoir
Thanks so much	Merçí beaucoup
Yes	Oui
No	Non
Pleased to meet you . .	Enchanté
How much is this? . . .	C'est combien?
Please.	S'il vous plait
Go Monaco!	Allez Monaco!

Many of the etiquette rules in Monaco are very similar to the rules of etiquette in French. However, assuming that Monegasque people are French often is not well received. Keep in mind that the city-state has its own history, culture, people, and language as well.

It may be considered rude to be very loud in a public or crowded place in Monaco. Many people talk relatively quietly.

INTERNET LINKS

en.gouv.mc/Government-Institutions/History-and-Heritage/Symbols/Monegasque-language
The website of Monaco's government gives an overview of the Monegasque language.

www.monaco-tribune.com/en/2020/04/umparamu-u-munegascu-discovering-the-monegasque-language/
This article shares a little more about the history of the Monegasque language.

theculturetrip.com/europe/monaco/articles/10-monegasque-phrases-to-know-before-visiting-monaco/
Learn some Monegasque phrases that would be commonly used in Monaco.

ARTS

Dancers of Les Ballets de Monte-Carlo take part in a performance in 2019 at the Grimaldi Forum Monaco.

10

THE CITY-STATE OF MONACO IS fairly dedicated to the arts, with galleries, art festivals, music and dance schools and venues, and unique architecture and sculpture abounding. Because so many residents and visitors are wealthy, even the priciest art is often available for sale or viewing. There are many performances of varying kinds to watch and listen to, as well as beautiful, unique buildings to visit.

The royals of Monaco have supported the arts for generations. In fact, a number of them have started art foundations and festivals that continue today.

PERFORMANCE ART

The famous Monte Carlo Casino was designed by French architect Charles Garnier, and it includes the Salle Garnier, an elaborate red and gold structure that is home to the Monte-Carlo Opera, Les Ballets de Monte-Carlo, and the 100-member Monte-Carlo Philharmonic Orchestra. The building, which has been renovated over the years, was inaugurated with a performance by the renowned Sarah Bernhardt in 1879, and it has welcomed guest artists including Enrico Caruso in the early 1900s and more contemporary singers such as Luciano Pavarotti, Plácido Domingo,

The Monte-Carlo Opera House is one of Monaco's most famous buildings.

and Andrea Bocelli. The Ballet Russes de Monte-Carlo, a company formed before Les Ballets de Monte-Carlo, has also seen performances by major dancers of the past few centuries. Famous composers, such as Igor Stravinsky, have written pieces for it, and sets have been designed by artists such as Jean Cocteau and Pablo Picasso.

The Monte-Carlo Philharmonic Orchestra usually performs in the Monte-Carlo Opera House, but in summer, it plays in the Palace Courtyard. The orchestra also acts as one of Monaco's goodwill ambassadors by playing in other countries.

A boys' choir also represents Monaco to the rest of the world. The choir, named Les Petits Chanteurs de Monaco (the Little Singers of Monaco) was originally formed by Prince Antoine I in the early 18th century to sing liturgical music in the Palatine Chapel. Prince Rainier III revived the choir in the early 1970s. It consists of about 30 young singers from Monaco, France, and Italy. Twice a year, the boys go on tours of other countries. For most of the year, they sing at 10 a.m. Mass at the cathedral.

Throughout the year, visitors and Monegasques enjoy a wide variety of music in addition to the classical forms. During the summer months, for example, the Monte Carlo Sporting Club holds concerts by internationally known recording stars. Now in its 48th year, the club's past performers have included David Bowie, Cher, Natalie Cole, and the Beach Boys.

Numerous other concerts are held during the year, such as "Jazz on the Rock," which is held in September. In addition, several clubs offer live jazz every evening, while others have rock groups or dance bands.

Another annual event is the Monte-Carlo Spring Arts Festival, usually held in April. The event includes classical and modern dance performances, concerts, and recitals. Events are held in numerous places and public squares, as well as the Grimaldi Forum Monaco.

MONEGASQUE ARTISTS

The Monegasque community does not have many well-known artists, likely due to the small size of the population, but there are some. Philibert (Philippe Antoine Vincent) Florence was a painter and illustrator born in Monaco in 1839 to a family full of artists. He redid and created frescoes in the Prince's Palace, and he created many paintings and drawings. He also taught young artists. Francois Joseph Bosio was a Monegasque sculptor who worked for Napoleon and the rulers of France.

More modern artists include painter Claude Gauthier, painter and sculptor Philippe Pastor, and Dutch-Monegasque sculptor Adeline de Monseignat. Artist Zoia Skoropadenko, though born in the Ukraine, works in Monaco and owns a gallery there. Emma de Sigaldi was a sculptor and dancer who was born in Germany and worked in Monaco.

OTHER ARTS

The streets, gardens, and public squares of Monaco are often filled with beautiful colors and the sounds of many musical forms. Contributing to this feast for the senses are many beautiful buildings and striking fountains and sculptural works. In addition to the buildings designed by Charles Garnier, there are splendid villas, churches, palaces, and forts. Some structures have been modernized from their original form. The 18th-century Fort Antoine has become a popular theater that hosts a wide range of productions in summer.

Part of the interior of the Palatine Chapel is shown here.

The construction of Monaco's cathedral began in 1875 and continued over a 10-year period. It is built out of Italian marble, creating a massive cream-colored façade. It is famous for its ancient altarpiece and for being the burial place of many members of the royal family, including Princess Grace. A much smaller church, the Palatine Chapel, was originally built in the 13th century as the Chapel of Saint John the Baptist. It is known for its strikingly beautiful ceiling painting and stained-glass windows.

Other well-known buildings include the Prince's Palace, the National Museum (also designed by Garnier), the glass-walled Grimaldi Forum Monaco (with more than half the structure submerged beneath the surface of the sea), and the Oceanographic Museum, with its façade rising from a sheer cliff.

Monaco is also full of striking sculptures, many of them outdoors and on display in gardens. Outside the Oceanographic Museum, for example, the steep paths of the Saint Martin Gardens are studded with sculptures. The central strip of the Casino Garden serves a similar function, and the Princess Grace Rose Garden devotes a large pathway called Chemin des Sculptures (Sculpture Road) to sculptures, including some that are part of Monaco's permanent collection.

Sculptures can be found throughout the small city-state of Monaco.

ON THE SCREEN

In 1961, Prince Rainier III launched the first Monte Carlo Television Festival. In his introduction, the prince said that the purpose of the event was to "encourage a new form of artistic expression in the service of peace and understanding for mankind." The gathering was a pioneering effort, as regular television broadcasting had started barely a decade earlier.

Part of Rainier's plan was to add to Monaco's status in the world as a cultural leader. Television was seen as a way of bringing nations and cultures together and helping them acquire mutual understanding. The event was a success and continues today, with many celebrities sitting on juries to judge the best in television programming.

Many movies have been shot, in full or in part, in Monaco. Perhaps the best known are some of the James Bond movies, including *Never Say Never Again* and *Goldeneye*. Others include *To Catch a Thief* (starring Cary Grant and Grace Kelly, who would go on to marry Prince Rainier III and become Monaco's princess), *Grand Prix*, and *Iron Man 2*.

HELPING HANDS (AND FUNDS)

Foundations created by Monaco's royal family have helped arts in the city-state for years. The Princess Grace Foundation was formed by the princess in 1964 to provide aid to the arts while also supporting medical and social programs. The foundation funds the Princess Grace Dance Academy, with classes and experimental performances. Another activity supported by the foundation is the Princess Grace Irish Library. In 1996, Prince Rainier III organized the Prince Pierre Foundation in honor of his father. This foundation awards several annual prizes, including the annual Grand Literary Prize, the Prince Rainier III Prize for Musical Composition, and the International Contemporary Art Prize. Another royal foundation is the Prince Rainier Musical Academy Foundation, which promotes new and even experimental pieces and awards the Musical Composition Prize.

INTERNET LINKS

www.hellomonaco.com/sightseeing/history-pages/famous-monegasques-remembering-philibert-florence-the-great-artist-from-monaco/
You can learn more about Philibert Florence in this article.

www.imdb.com/name/nm0860019/bio
Danièle Thompson's Internet Movie Database biography also links to a list of her movies.

www.tvfestival.com/en
The website of the Monte Carlo Television Festival has more information on this annual event.

www.visitmonaco.com/us/place/promenade/88/sculptures-trails
Visit Monaco offers information on the Chemin des Sculptures here.

Danièle Thompson is a Monegasque filmmaker who's been nominated for an Academy Award. Acclaimed writer and filmmaker Armand Gatti was also born in Monaco.

LEISURE

Families do the same things for fun in Monaco that they do in other places around the world—like visit carnivals and other events.

11

Visitors can ask questions and pick up maps and brochures for activities and entertainment at Monaco's Tourism Office.

AS A TOURIST DESTINATION WITH many resorts and millions of visitors a year, it is not surprising that Monaco has many leisure activities available. There are places to relax, places to be active, places to shop, places to watch performances, places to learn, and, of course, places to gamble.

Both wealthy residents and visitors expect to spend a lot of money to enjoy themselves, and leisure activities can be very expensive. On a typical day, for instance, a well-to-do couple might first spend time (and money) visiting exclusive designer shops in the neighborhood known as the Carré d'Or (Golden Square). They might then dine among the posh 17th-century décor of the Louis XV restaurant, said to be the finest on the entire Riviera, followed by a pampering at a luxury spa, featuring a rose-scented massage. The evening could be spent at the fabled Monte Carlo Casino, where formal attire (and a good deal of money) is required.

At the other end of the economic scale, however, there are activities available that cost a good deal less money. One could attend a public concert at one of Monaco's parks, then dine on slices of pizza from the Casino Supermarket while strolling through the Chemin des Sculptures in the Princess Grace Rose Garden. After a visit to any of the museums, visitors may choose to have a picnic with fresh foods from Monaco's covered market on the waterfront and, as the sun goes down, enjoy a display of fireworks over the harbor.

MOVIES AND FESTIVALS

Music, dance, and theater programs make up part of the entertainment listings available in Monaco. Movie theaters, although few in number, are also popular. In summer, the Open-Air Cinema, which boasts the largest outdoor screen in all of Europe, shows English-language films. Monegasques are particularly fond of movies, and a number of films have been shot there. In addition, many Hollywood personalities vacation in Monaco or nearby, especially when the prestigious Cannes Film Festival is in progress.

A variety of festivals offer different forms of entertainment throughout the year. The International Pyromelodic Fireworks Competition fills the night sky in July and August with displays of fireworks by the leading pyrotechnic specialists from many countries. The International Circus Festival arrives in January. Just about every month of the year offers yet another festival.

AMAZING RACE

The principality offers many events for spectators, but the most famous is the Monaco Grand Prix. The Formula One Grand Prix trophy is one that is most coveted by drivers, and the Monaco race may be the most glamorous one on the circuit. In 2021, it was part of a series made up of 23 Formula One races held on five continents, leading to the finale in Abu Dhabi.

On a Sunday in late May, the air in Monaco is filled with the smell of high-powered fuel and burning rubber, as well as the roar of engines and the screeching of tires. The cars race through the very heart of the city, going uphill from the start/finish line to the casino, then streaking downhill around a tight hairpin turn and two other sharp turns and through a tunnel, along the harbor, navigating more sharp turns that lead back to the start/finish line. The cars have to run through this course 77 times before the race is considered complete.

Spectators watch the excitement from terrace restaurants or from people's homes, while the wealthy enjoy the comforts of the Hôtel Hermitage or view the race from luxury yachts in the harbor. The Grimaldis and their guests have a royal box at the port.

In terms of races, the Monaco Grand Prix is not considered to be one of the greatest by experts. For one thing, the course is too tight and tricky for the big Formula One cars, which are built for speed rather than sharp turns. The average speed is only 88 miles (about 142 km) per hour. Also, because of the many tight turns and steep hills, it is almost impossible to pass another car.

The audience waits for the cars to appear at the Monaco Grand Prix.

Still, perhaps no other race can compare with the Monaco Grand Prix for sheer excitement and glamour. For the spectators, the speed certainly does not seem too slow. In fact, until stronger barriers were erected, there were two times when cars plowed through the straw bales and into the harbor. (On both occasions, the drivers suffered only minor injuries.)

Many Formula One drivers make Monaco their permanent home. They include some of the most famous personalities in the racing world, including Emanuele Pirro and Mika Pauli Häkkinen.

FOR CAR ENTHUSIASTS

The fascination with cars is not limited to the Monaco Grand Prix. The Monte Carlo Rally, held in January every year, is another famous event. This is a three-day race, held in timed stages, which begins and ends in Monaco. In between, it follows a tortuous route through Provence in France. The winding mountain roads above Monaco are sometimes clogged with snow.

January and February also witness the Monte Carlo Historic Car Rally. Historic sports cars take part in a race that begins in France in Valence, then follows a challenging course, with a pause in Gap, and finishes in Monaco.

Prince Rainier III was a race car buff and a collector of historic cars. More than 100 of his vehicles are on display at the Collection de Voitures Anciennes (Collection of Classic Cars). The collection includes the Bugatti 1929, the winner of the first Monaco Grand Prix.

A LOVE OF SPORTS

Prince Rainier III once said, "To be a true Monegasque, you must have a love of sports." Monaco offers a seemingly endless variety of sports. Here is a sampling.

BOATING AND BEACH ACTIVITIES   Monaco's harbor is filled with a wide array of sailboats and yachts. There are numerous luxury yachts, and many are anchored at the members-only Monaco Yacht Club. All sorts of motor craft and sailboats enjoy the calm waters and magnificent views. Visitors can take tours in a glass-bottomed catamaran operated by a tour company. The

adventurous can try deep-sea fishing for tuna or join a sailboat race. Those who prefer observing or sightseeing can take a helicopter tour of the entire coast.

The Rainier III Nautical Stadium hosts Olympic-quality swimming races. A number of European and world records have been set here. Water polo matches and beach volleyball are also popular.

A member of a crew takes part in a yacht race in Monaco in 2019.

TENNIS AND GOLF   Visitors and full-time residents take advantage of Monaco's many tennis courts. People play for pleasure, to keep in shape, and to take part in a variety of amateur competitions.

In the spring of every year, the Monte Carlo Country Club (which is actually just outside Monaco in France) hosts the Tennis Masters Series. The best players in men's tennis compete in an event that celebrated its 100th edition in 2006.

Young people play soccer in an open space in Monte Carlo.

The Masters Series ranks second only to the Grand Slam in importance and prestige. The series consists of tournaments in North America, Europe, and Asia.

The Monte Carlo Pro-Celebrity PGA Golf Tournament is the major golfing event held at the Monte Carlo Golf Club. Professional golfers are paired with famous entertainers, including film stars. People who simply want to play golf at the Monte Carlo Golf Club need to make reservations a year or two in advance.

TEAM SPORTS   Of the team sports, football (soccer) is by far the most popular. Young people play wherever they can find space, while the ultramodern, 20,000-seat Louis II Stadium in Fontvieille is a venue for European Junior and French First Division matches. The Monegasque National Team is the pride and joy of the principality. In their red-and-white uniforms, the players come from France, Italy, and Monaco, as well as other countries.

Other sports for watching or playing include bicycle races, squash, gymnastics, and handball. The Monaco Sports Association (ASM) works to develop interest in several other sports organizations, including the Archery Company, the Monaco Rifle Club, the Monaco Cycling Union, and, for rowers, the Société Nautique de Monaco.

PÉTANQUE Throughout the Riviera, including Monaco, the game called *pétanque* or *boules* is wildly popular. The Italian game of boccie (or bocce) is quite similar. The game, with two to six players divided into two teams, is played on a level gravel course. Each player has three boules, or balls, made of solid metal, that weigh somewhere between 1 and 2 pounds (0.5 and 1 kg). Each team takes a turn rolling a boule at a small wooden ball called a *cochonnet* (jack), trying to land their boule as close to the cochonnet as possible. The team with the closest boule wins the round and earns one point. The first team to earn 13 points wins the match.

The toss is always made underhand from inside a small circle scratched in the gravel. Both of the player's feet are firmly planted on the ground. At the end of a round, a new circle is drawn around the cochonnet and the boules must be rolled from 6.6 to 11 yards (6 to 10 m) farther away.

There is now an international federation of pétanque national associations. There are more than 500,000 players registered, representing about 50 countries, including Canada and the United States. The world championship is often held in Monaco's Rainier III Boules Stadium.

OLYMPIC CONNECTIONS AND OTHERS

Prince Rainier III and now Prince Albert II have devoted a good deal of energy and creativity to making their tiny principality stand out in the world of sports. Prince Albert, for example, has served on the International Olympic Committee for several years and was also captain of Monaco's bobsled team in four Winter Olympics. His wife, Princess Charlene, was an Olympic swimmer for South Africa.

Under the leadership of Prince Rainier III, Monaco encouraged several international sports organizations to establish headquarters in the city-state.

As of early 2021, Monaco has not yet won an Olympic medal, although the country has taken part in most Summer Olympics since 1920 and every Winter Olympics since 1984.

> ## BEACH LIFE
>
> *Larvotto beach is Monaco's only public beach, and as such, it tends to be very popular. Admission is free, although lounge chairs can be rented—and since it has small pebbles instead of sand, that might be a good idea. The water tends to be shallow and calm, so it's especially popular with families. Bars and restaurants of various price levels are scattered about. A watersports center provides rentals and activities such as parasailing, as well as a nearby beach volleyball court. There are also lifeguards on duty and even a special jellyfish net to keep them away during the summer.*

The Oceanographic Museum is perched right at the edge of the Mediterranean Sea in Monaco.

These organizations include the International Association for Sport Without Violence. Rainier helped to create the association and served as its president. In total, Monaco's Department of the Interior oversees the work of more than 50 sports organizations, many of which provide financial aid to promote various sports.

PLACES TO LEARN

Both residents and visitors can spend leisure hours in Monaco's museums and public gardens. The National Museum is located in a grand villa designed by Charles Garnier. It includes a huge doll collection and mechanical toys. Nearby, the Naval Museum showcases more than 200 model ships. There is also an elaborate gondola that was built for the Emperor Napoleon. The Prince's Palace has more Napoleon-related items on display in the Museé des Souvenirs Napoléoniens et Archives Historiques du Palais (Musuem of Napoleonic Souvenirs and the Historic Archives of the Palace).

The Wax Museum of the Princes of Monaco offers 24 life-size figures in historic scenes of the Grimaldi family's history. A few steps away is a 17th-century chapel called the Musée de la Chapelle de la Visitation (Museum of the Chapel of the Visitation) in which classic artwork is displayed.

The Oceanographic Museum is one of Monaco's most famous sites. Even the décor is sea-themed, including chandeliers shaped like seabirds and oak doorframes carved into marine shapes. The Whale Room contains skeletons and preserved specimens of whales and marine creatures. Outside the museum, the plants of the Jardins Saint Martin cover the steep hillsides above the coast. The garden includes a number of statues, as well as breathtaking views.

Of course, Monegasques also do all the same leisure activities as people elsewhere in the world. They watch TV and read, meet friends for fun and meals, listen to music, travel, cook, and enjoy the outdoors.

People lounge on the beach in Monaco, right by the blue waters of the Mediterranean Sea.

INTERNET LINKS

www.formula1monaco.com/
The official Formula One website provides information about the Monaco Grand Prix.

www.travelchannel.com/interests/beaches/articles/larvotto-beach-and-monte-carlo
This Travel Channel website gives more details about Monaco's Larvotto beach and nearby attractions.

www.tripadvisor.com/Attractions-g190405-Activities-zft11292-Monaco.html
TripAdvisor lists its top 10 free things to do in Monaco on this website.

www.visitmonaco.com/us
The official Monaco tourism website has a wealth of knowledge about the city-state and things to do there.

FESTIVALS

The International Circus Festival of Monte Carlo is one of the city-state's most popular and famous festivals.

12

The Côte d'Azur Gardens Festival is one of the region's newer festivals. It took place for the first time in 2017.

MONACO IS KNOWN FOR ITS SHEER number of festivals and celebrations. These start in January with one of the city-state's most unique events and continue right through the year until the festivities at Christmas. They involve or are focused on fireworks, gardens, national pride, the arts, television, film, and more.

There are at least two reasons for the many festivals. For one thing, who doesn't love a good party? An event that combines parades, music, colorful costumes, lots of food, and often fireworks has all the ingredients for a grand celebration. Another important reason for at least some of the festivals is that they provide a convenient way to bring visitors to Monaco, and, at the same time, they make the outside world aware of the small principality and its attractions.

Monaco's festivals are both religious and secular. Since more than 90 percent of the people are Catholic, religious celebrations like the Feast of Saint Dévote, as well as more universal celebrations such as Easter, can involve large numbers. The secular festivals, such as the circus or the fireworks festivals, are likely to attract hundreds of additional visitors.

Monaco's Princess
Stéphanie and her
daughter Pauline
Ducruet pose with
performers before
the International
Circus Festival
in 2017.

CIRCUS TIME!

Every January, the best circus troupes in the world are invited to compete in
the International Circus Festival of Monte Carlo, one of the most popular affairs
of the year. A huge tent, with room for three rings and seating for thousands
of spectators, is set up in an area called the Espace Fontvieille.

More than 100 acts are entered in the competition, from acrobats and
trapeze troupes to lion tamers, elephant acts, and trained tigers. Performers
come from all parts of the world. Throughout the week, the international
stars compete for prizes in several categories. The winners receive little
statuettes called Clowns d'Ors (Golden Clowns), the circus world's equivalent
of Hollywood's Academy Awards statuette. The festival, which concludes with
the Gala Awards Show, is one of the most thrilling circus shows in the world.

GET READY FOR FIREWORKS

The International Fireworks Competition lights up the skies over Monaco nearly every summer.

Another Monaco event is the annual International Pyromelodic Fireworks Competition (or Art en Ciel), held almost every summer since 1966. (It was canceled in 2020 due to the COVID-19 pandemic.) As the Mediterranean skies darken each night, fireworks specialists from around the world compete with colorful and noisy displays of pyrotechnic skills. The show begins in July and continues through August.

The exciting display of fireworks can be watched from any number of venues, such as along the harbor, at outdoor cafés and terrace restaurants, the grounds of the palace, and along the ramparts of Fort Antoine. Every evening seems to offer a surprise or two, as specialists from Canada, China, the United States, Japan, Australia, and many parts of Europe vie for various

January 1.	*New Year's Day*
January	*International Circus Festival*
. . . .	*Feast of Saint Dévote*
February and March . . .	*Carnival*
March/April	*Easter Sunday and Monday*
May 1.	*May Day or Workers' Day*
May.	*Feast of the Ascension*
May/June.	*Pentecost/Whitsunday and Whitmonday*
June.	*Feast of Saint John*
. . . .	*Monaco Festival of the Sea*
July/August.	*International Fireworks Festival*
August	*Feast of the Assumption*
November 1	*All Saints' Day*
November 19.	*National Day (Fete Nationale)*
December 8	*Feast of the Immaculate Conception*
December 25	*Christmas*

prizes. The winning team returns in November for a display on the eve of Monaco's National Day, November 19.

FOR LOVE OF THE SEA

Although Monaco's harbor is best known for its luxury yachts, the Fête de la Mer (Festival of the Sea) is quite different. Instead of big yachts (some with their own pools and helicopter pads), the bay is filled one day every June with fishing boats, sailing vessels, and motorboats. The event celebrates Saint Peter, the patron saint of sailors.

The mixed regatta files through the port for blessings, followed by an array of activities. All classes of sailboats can take part in races, some of which are open to amateurs and others to professionals. There are also displays of different crafts and accessories.

NATIONAL PRIDE

National Day, which is also known as the Feast of the Prince, is held each year, preceded by the award-winning fireworks display the evening before. National Day is a festive affair, with people in traditional Monegasque costumes taking part in a colorful parade to the palace. There is plenty of music, traditional folk dances, and a variety of foods. The prince makes a public appearance and spends part of the day greeting visitors.

The day of the festival is traditionally picked by the reigning prince. Prince Albert II choose November 19 as the day of the festival to honor his father, Prince Rainier III, as it marks the feast day of his father's namesake saint.

Prince Jacques and Princess Gabriella of Monaco wave flags during Monaco's National Day in 2019.

The prince and other members of the royal family also play important parts in a number of other annual events. In March, they host the Rose Ball, a charity affair, followed in August by the Red Cross Gala Ball. Held in the Monaco Sporting Club, the Red Cross Gala Ball is one of the largest charity events in Europe. It brings together the social elite of the continent. The prince also hosts a picnic for the people of Monaco every June.

CELEBRATING THE ARTS

A number of festivals also celebrate various forms of the arts every year. The Spring Arts Festival takes place in the spring in locations throughout Monaco, while the International Festival of Amateur Theatre celebrates community and amateur theater and takes place every four years. The Monaco Film Festival takes place annually, awarding the Angel Film Awards for nonviolent films, and the Monaco Charity Film Festival raises money for disadvantaged children around the world. The Monte Carlo Jazz Festival is another annual event, celebrating jazz music and its diversity.

Princess Grace founded both the Rose Ball and Monaco's Spring Arts Festival.

INTERNET LINKS

www.monaco-feuxdartifice.mc/en
The official website of the Monaco Art en Ciel (fireworks competition) offers more information about the event.

www.monacofilmfest.com/
The Monaco International Film Festival website has many photographs of past winners.

www.montecarlofestival.mc/en/
The Monte Carlo International Circus Festival site has event information and lists of past winners.

yacht-club-monaco.mc/en/events/fete-de-la-mer/
This website devoted to Monaco's Fête de la Mer has schedules and photos of the event.

FOOD

Monegasque cuisine tends to use lots of fresh, local produce, such as that shown here.

13

WITH ITS SPOT ON THE CÔTE d'Azur, right near France and Italy, Monaco has a native cuisine that is influenced by both regions. There is lots of fresh seafood and the usual Mediterranean ingredients of olive oil, olives, fresh produce, garlic, herbs, and nuts. The city-state's open-air markets provide plentiful fresh ingredients. Also, because of the many people from different countries now living in Monaco, there is much access to more international foods and dishes at restaurants, ranging from relatively inexpensive to incredibly pricey and luxurious.

There is a big insistence on freshness in ingredients, partly a product of history—until the age of modern transportation, local products were not transported very far. As a result, people learned to rely on the farm and fishing products of their area. Traditionally, for example, men on fishing boats from the Marseille region began preparing their famous bouillabaisse (fish stew) while the boat was sailing toward port. Today, a popular Monaco restaurant guarantees that fish, ordered for the midday meal, will have arrived within the past two hours from the sea.

The Monte-Carlo Gastronomie, an international food fair, takes place every November in Monaco.

A stand in a Christmas market in Monaco sells hot potatoes, a favorite from France.

COOKING IN MONACO

Traditional meal preparation can be time-consuming because prepared foods are rarely used. However, this sort of cooking is also simple in ways, as recipes do not require complicated sauces or heavy seasoning. Many people eat their main meal at midday, but the requirements of most modern jobs make this increasingly difficult. This has led to a growing trend toward evening dining. On holidays and other festive occasions, people usually gather with friends and family for more elaborate meals. These meals can last two to three hours.

The people of Monaco sometimes shop every day or two in order to have the freshest foods possible. A simple breakfast might require a trip to a neighborhood bakery, for example, to purchase a baguette (a long, pointed

Barbajuan *(also spelled* barbagiuan*), which is also popular in France and Italy, is Monaco's national dish. These crunchy, fried appetizers are generally stuffed with ricotta cheese and Swiss chard, although other ingredients (including garlic, herbs, rice, onion, and other kinds of cheese) are often used as well. Many families have their own unique recipe. In the Monegasque language, its name means "Uncle John," and it is particularly eaten on Monaco's National Day, November 19. A Roca, an organization that promotes the cuisine of the Riviera, sometimes hosts a barbajuan festival—and has a mascot called "BarbaChef" that is actually a humanoid barbajuan.*

loaf of bread) that is still a little warm from the oven. To ensure its freshness, the clerk does not put the loaf in a bag; instead, a piece of paper is wrapped around the middle of the bread for carrying it. Freshly squeezed orange juice and freshly brewed coffee would complete the meal, along with butter and jam for the bread and milk for the coffee. On some mornings, the baguette might be replaced with croissants (buttery, crescent-shaped rolls) or pain au chocolat (puff pastry filled with chocolate).

Shopping for the evening meal might be accomplished after work, with a stroll through the shaded stalls of an open-air market. Shoppers fill their baskets with fresh vegetables: tomatoes, cucumbers, onions, green beans, green peppers, and young potatoes. At home, they might cut these up, add ground fresh tuna, hard-boiled eggs, and anchovies, then top the ingredients with an olive oil—based dressing to make a salade nicoise, a creation from the next-door city of Nice. Dessert for this meal might be a local cantaloupe to serve with *navettes*, cookies flavored with anise and orange blossom.

POPULAR DISHES

Monaco has a number of popular regional dishes, including the national dish, barbajuan, a sort of stuffed fritter; gnocchi, small potato dumplings; *porchetta*, a pork roast; *fougasse*, a flatbread; *socca*, crepes made of chickpea flour;

Socca is a popular street food in Monaco, although it originated in France.

Cooks might shop for fresh vegetables in Monaco's open-air markets to make the vegetarian dish ratatouille, shown here.

pan bagnat, a sandwich with eggs, vegetables, and anchovies; and *stocafi*, a fish stew.

More generally speaking, many vegetables are popular with Monegasques. They can be served with rice or pasta or on their own. Some of the most popular ingredients are combined in a standard dish called ratatouille. This includes staples such as onions, eggplant (aubergine), zucchini, green peppers, and artichokes stewed together with tomatoes, garlic, and herbs.

Fresh vegetables can also be cut up and served raw as crudités with a dip such as anchovy paste mixed with garlic and olive oil. Stuffed vegetables are also popular, such as eggplant stuffed with ground or chopped meat, onions, and herbs, served in a tomato sauce.

Some soups are hearty enough to be self-contained meals. *Soupe de poisson* (fish soup), for instance, made with fresh fish, is served with crisp toast, a

Bouillabaisse, a fish stew, is popular in Monaco.

clove of garlic, and rouille, a spicy mayonnaise made with crushed chili peppers. *Soupe au pistou* is a thick, minestrone-like vegetable soup, served with pistou—a sauce made with garlic, basil, and olive oil—stirred into it.

Monegasques and other long-term Monaco residents are more likely to prepare seafood than meat. The variety of freshly caught fish is almost endless, but the most popular are probably sea bass, tuna, red snapper, mullet, anchovy, and cod. The most common meat is lamb, which is usually roasted with herbs. Beef is most popular in slow-cooked stews, called *daubes*, but is rarely seen as steaks or roasts. In the past, wild game, such as rabbit, wild boar, and birds, was popular, but the decline of hunting has made game much less common in meals.

Fresh fruit is always popular, especially for use in desserts, and the region abounds with excellent varieties of fruit: oranges and lemons from Menton;

Cavaillon melons and cherries from Luberon; and apricots, table grapes, and figs from various locations. The region is not famous for cheese, which is unusual since both France and Italy are known for their cheeses. Probably the best known is Banon goat cheese, a nutty goat cheese made in small disks that are individually wrapped in chestnut leaves and tied with raffia. In addition to fruit, popular desserts include custards, such as crème brulee, various fruit tarts, and all sorts of pastries. Ice cream is also common. The local favorite is a delicate chestnut ice cream.

RESTAURANTS

Monaco is famous for its four- and five-star restaurants, including two or three that are regarded as among the finest on the Mediterranean coast. As is the case with most modern cities, visitors can find just about all of the world's major cuisines. Monaco's restaurants tend to feature Italian and French recipes, and they rely heavily on seasonal foods, such as young asparagus in the spring, zucchinis and eggplant in summer, and figs and pumpkins in the fall. Pasta

People eat on the terrace of the Café de Paris Monte-Carlo in Monaco.

dishes are very popular—spaghetti, ravioli, and all sorts of small pastas. Some northern Italian recipes are based on rice. Even some of the great chefs use simple recipes, and most avoid the rich, creamy sauces of northern France.

Perhaps the most notable restaurant in Monaco is Le Louis XV, an Alain Ducasse restaurant with three Michelin stars, located in the Hôtel de Paris. Other starred restaurants include Le Vistamar, a seafood-focused restaurant with a beautiful terrace; Le Blue Bay, which blends Mediterranean and Caribbean cuisines; Yoshi, which features Japanese cuisine; and Elsa, the first all-organic restaurant to get a Michelin star.

The Café de Paris Monte-Carlo, right across from the Place du Casino, is great for meals as well as people watching. The historic Condamine Market, which has been open for the past 140 years, is a sort of an upscale food court featuring traders with food, flowers, and more. It is a good place to get fresh, authentic Monegasque foods.

INTERNET LINKS

www.aroca.mc/
A Roca's website offers a great deal of information on the cuisine of the French Riviera, including Monaco.

montecarlogastronomie.com/en/
The website of the Monte-Carlo Gastronomie contains more information about the foodie event.

www.montecarlosbm.com/en/restaurant-monaco/le-louis-xv-alain-ducasse-hotel-de-paris
Investigate the famed Le Louis XV restaurant, including menus and history, on this web page.

theculturetrip.com/europe/monaco/articles/a-brief-history-of-barbagiuan-monacos-national-dish/
Learn more about barbajuan from this Culture Trip article.

BARBAJUAN

For the pastry:
1 ¼ cup flour
A dash of salt
About 3 tablespoons plus 1 teaspoon olive oil
One egg, beaten
About 3 tablespoons plus 1 teaspoon water
Oil for frying

For the filling:
1 tablespoon olive oil
¼ cup finely chopped onion
¼ cup leeks (white parts), chopped
Pinch of dried oregano
2 Swiss chard leaves (green parts), chopped
⅓ to ½ cup fresh spinach, chopped
⅓ to ½ cup ricotta cheese
¼ cup Parmesan cheese
1 egg white, beaten

First, prepare the pastry. Stir the flour and salt together. Add the olive oil and half the egg; stir. (Save the rest of the egg.) Add just enough water to make a firm dough. Turn on to a floured surface, and knead for 5 minutes. Cover in plastic wrap, and chill for about 30 minutes.

Next, prepare the filling. Heat the olive oil in a frying pan over medium heat. Add the onion and leek, and cook about 5 minutes. Add the oregano, chard, and spinach, and cook about 10 minutes. Transfer to a bowl, and mix in the cheeses and the leftover egg from the pastry. Season with salt and pepper. Let cool.

Finally, put it all together. Turn the dough out onto a floured surface again and roll out to about 0.75 inch (2 centimeters) thick. Use a floured round cookie cutter and cut as many circles as you can. Reroll the dough and cut again until you have about 20 circles.

Put one teaspoon of filling in the center of every circle. Brush the edges with the egg white, then fold over and press the edges with a fork to seal. Transfer to a baking tray lined with foil. Pour oil into a deep pan (at least 1.5 inches/3.8 cm of oil), and heat until hot enough for deep frying. (This should always be done by an adult.) Transfer the semicircles to the oil, and fry about 5 minutes, until crisp. Remove onto a plate covered in a kitchen towel or paper towels using a slotted spoon.

SOCCA

1 cup chickpea flour
1 cup (237 milliliters) water
½ teaspoon sea salt
1 ¾ tablespoons extra virgin
   olive oil, divided
You will also need a 10-inch
   (25.4 cm) cast-iron skillet

Preheat the oven to 475ºF with the skillet inside. In a medium bowl, combine the first three ingredients and 1 tablespoon of the olive oil, and whisk until smooth. Cover and set aside for 30 minutes.

Using a pot holder, remove the skillet from the hot oven. Brush the remaining olive oil over the sides and bottom of the skillet. Pour the batter into the pan. Then, bake for 17 to 20 minutes, until brown and crisp around the edges. Remove from the oven and let cool, then use a spatula to transfer the socca from the pan to a serving plate.

Cut into wedges.

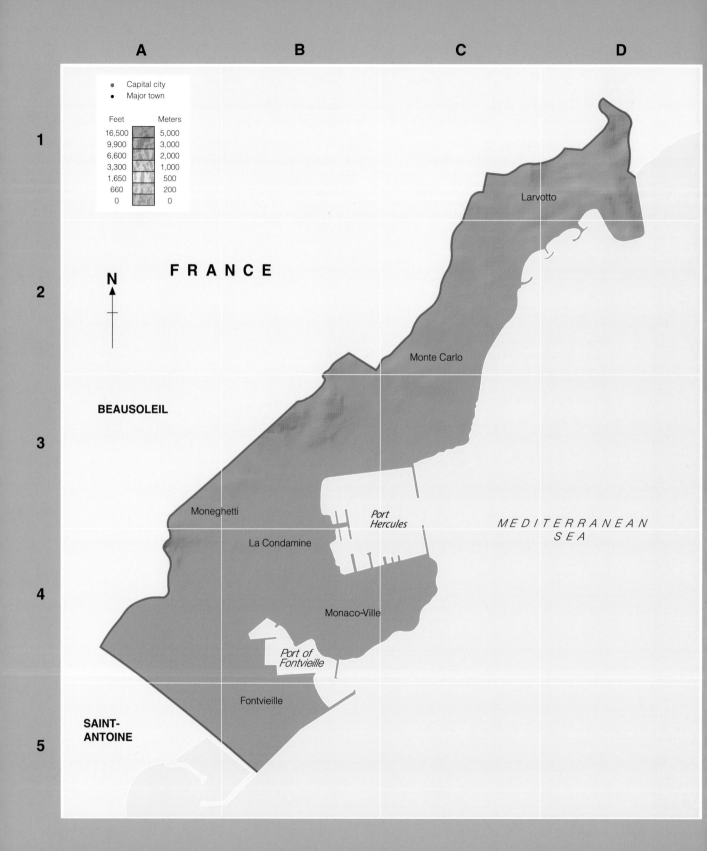

A   B   C   D

- Capital city
- Major town

Feet	Meters
16,500	5,000
9,900	3,000
6,600	2,000
3,300	1,000
1,650	500
660	200
0	0

1

FRANCE

N

2

BEAUSOLEIL

3

Larvotto

Monte Carlo

Moneghetti

Port Hercules

La Condamine

MEDITERRANEAN SEA

4

Monaco-Ville

Port of Fontvieille

Fontvieille

SAINT-ANTOINE

5

MAP OF MONACO

ECONOMIC MONACO

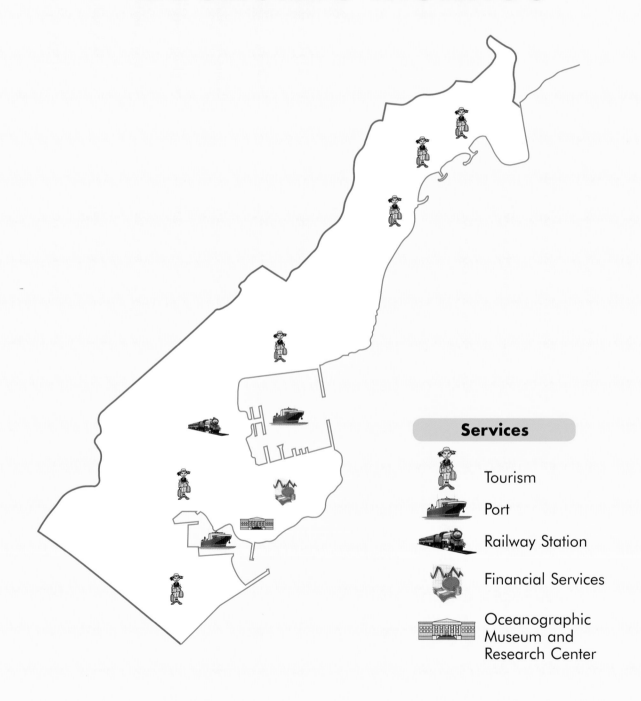

Services

Tourism

Port

Railway Station

Financial Services

Oceanographic Museum and Research Center

ABOUT THE ECONOMY

All figures are 2019 estimates unless otherwise noted.

GROSS DOMESTIC PRODUCT (GDP)
$7.9 billion (U.S.)

GDP GROWTH RATE
7.5 percent

PER CAPITA INCOME
$60,794 (Monegasques)

WORKFORCE
57,867

UNEMPLOYMENT RATE
About 2 percent

POPULATION BELOW POVERTY LINE
0 percent reported

LAND AREA
0.8 square miles (2 sq km)

LAND USE
agricultural land: 0 percent

CURRENCY
euro
$1 USD = 0.84 euro (2021)

AGRICULTURAL PRODUCTS
none

NATURAL RESOURCES
none

INDUSTRIES
tourism, services, construction, small-scale consumer products, banking

MAJOR TRADE PARTNERS
France, Italy, England, United States, Spain, Germany, Switzerland, Belgium

CULTURAL MONACO

Prince's Palace
This is the royal residence.

Jardin Exotique
Thousands of varieties of plants are in this spectacular cliffside garden.

The Grimaldi Forum Monaco
This beautiful glass building, partly below the sea, is used for conventions and exhibits.

Monte Carlo Casino
This famous casino is known for its elaborate architecture, as well as the world's most famous gambling tables.

Observatory Cave
This cave system has very early paintings.

Oceanographic Museum
It contains many tanks of tropical fish, plus a coral reef. The lower level has research facilities.

Princess Grace Rose Garden
Thousands of rose bushes were planted in memory of Princess Grace.

Saint Nicholas Cathedral
Built in 1875, the cathedral is the burial place of Prince Rainier III and Princess Grace.

ABOUT THE CULTURE

All figures are 2019 estimates unless otherwise noted.

OFFICAL NAME
Principality of Monaco

NATIONAL FLAG
two horizontal bands, with red on top, white on the bottom; the colors are from the Grimaldi coat of arms

MAJOR AREAS
Fontvieille, Monte Carlo, Moneghetti, La Condamine, Monaco-Ville

POPULATION
38,100 (2019)

POPULATION DENSITY
47,625 people per square mile
(19,050 per sq km)

ETHNIC GROUPS
French 25 percent, Monegasque
22.5 percent, Italian 19 percent, other
33.5 percent

LIFE EXPECTANCY
male 85.6 years, female 93.4 years

RELIGIOUS GROUPS
Roman Catholic more than 90 percent, others less than 10 percent

OFFICIAL LANGUAGE
French

EDUCATION
compulsory, ages 6 to 16

LITERACY RATE
99 percent

NATIONAL HOLIDAYS
Feast of Saint Dévote (January 27), National Day (November 19)

FAMOUS MONEGASQUES
Prince Albert I, explorer and ruler of Monaco (1848—1922)
Louis Notari, writer (1879—1961)
Princess Grace, movie star and princess (1929—1982)
Prince Rainier III, ruler of Monaco (1923—2005)
Prince Albert II, ruler of Monaco (1958—)

TIMELINE

IN MONACO	IN THE WORLD
600 BCE	
Greeks establish colony of Monoikos.	
125 BCE	
The Romans move in; Monaco is incorporated into the Roman Empire.	
300–310 CE	
Romans persecute Christians; Saint Dévote becomes a martyr.	
400–500 CE	
Tribes from the east invade the region.	**600 CE**
	The height of the Maya civilization is reached.
	1000
1215	The Chinese perfect gunpowder and
Genoa establishes a fort on the Rock of Monaco.	begin to use it in warfare.
1297	
François Grimaldi, disguised as a monk, seizes Monaco.	
1525	
Monaco is placed under the protection of Spain.	**1530**
	The beginning of the transatlantic slave trade is organized by the Portuguese in Africa.
	1558–1603
1612	The Reign of Elizabeth I of England takes place.
Honoré II is the first Grimaldi to	**1620**
take the title of prince of Monaco.	Pilgrims sail the *Mayflower* to America.
	1776
	U.S. Declaration of Independence is written.
	1789–1799
1793	The French Revolution takes place.
French take control of Monaco during the French Revolution. The Grimaldi family is imprisoned.	
1861	**1861**
Prince Charles III gives up Menton and Roquebrune to France in return for the independence of Monaco.	The American Civil War begins.
1863	
Gambling begins at the Monte Carlo Casino.	**1869**
	The Suez Canal is opened.

IN MONACO		IN THE WORLD
1911 Prince Albert I approves the first constitution.		
		1914 World War I begins.
1929 First Formula One Grand Prix race is held.		**1939** World War II begins.
		1945 The United States drops atomic bombs on Hiroshima and Nagasaki.
1949 Prince Rainier III begins his 56-year reign.		**1949** The North Atlantic Treaty Organization (NATO) is formed.
1956 Prince Rainier and Grace Kelly marry.		**1966–1969** The Chinese Cultural Revolution takes place.
1982 Princess Grace dies after a car crash.		
		1991 The breakup of the Soviet Union occurs.
1993 Monaco joins the United Nations.		**1997** Hong Kong is returned to China.
		2001 Terrorists crash planes in New York, Washington, D.C., and Pennsylvania.
2005 Prince Rainier III dies; Albert II becomes the ruling prince.		**2010** A huge earthquake devastates Hispaniola, especially Haiti.
2011 Prince Albert II marries Charlene Wittstock of South Africa.		
2014 Princess Gabriella and Hereditary Prince of Monaco Jacques are born.		**2015** The United States legalizes same-sex marriage.
		2019 U.S. president Donald Trump is impeached, though not removed from office. (He is impeached again in 2021.)
2020 Events such as the Grand Prix are canceled due to the COVID-19 pandemic. Monaco launches its first satellite.		**2020** The COVID-19 pandemic sweeps across the world.

GLOSSARY

Côte d'Azur
The Azure Coast, the Mediterranean coast of southern France and Monaco.

ecotourism
The practice of touring natural habitats and other places in a way meant to minimize ecological impact.

Kyoto Protocol
An international agreement to take vigorous steps to reduce the amount of greenhouse gases in the upper atmosphere. Monaco signed in 2005.

lifts
The word used in European countries for elevators.

Les Petits Chanteurs de Monaco
The Little Singers of Monaco, the principality's famous boys' choir.

Monegasques
The native-born citizens of Monaco, making up about 22.5 percent of the population.

Palladienne
A Monegasque folk group of singers and dancers.

pandemic
An event in which a disease spreads very quickly to a large amount of people over a wide area—or throughout the world.

principality
A small geographic area ruled by a prince.

proportional representation
A system of voting based on the percentage of votes received by each political party in the last election.

Saint Dévote
A Christian martyr who became the patron saint of Monaco.

tax haven
A place where people and companies go to avoid having to pay high taxes.

FOR FURTHER INFORMATION

BOOKS

Clark, Gregor, and Lonely Planet. *Nice and Monaco* (Lonely Planet Pocket). Franklin, TN: Lonely Planet Publications, 2019.

Hewett, Michael. *Monaco Grand Prix*. Somerset, UK: Haynes Publishing, 2007.

Hintz, Martin. *Monaco* (Enchantment of the World Series). New York, NY: Children's Press, 2004.

WEBSITES

Lonely Planet Monaco. www.lonelyplanet.com/monaco.

The Monaco Tribune. www.monaco-tribune.com/en/.

The Monegasque Institute of Statistics and Economic Studies. www.monacostatistics.mc/.

The Principality of Monaco (Official Website). en.gouv.mc/.

Visit Monaco. www.visitmonaco.com/us.

BIBLIOGRAPHY

Bell, Brian, ed. *French Riviera*. London, England: APA Publications, 2003.

Burgan, Michael. *Grace of Monaco*. New York, NY: Children's Press, 2020.

DK Eyewitness. *Provence and the Cote d'Azur*. London, England: DK Publishing, 2018.

Edwards, Anne. *The Grimaldis of Monaco: Centuries of Scandal, Years of Grace*. Guilford, CT: Lyons Press, 2017.

Facaros, Dana, and Michael Pauls. *South of France*. Guilford, CT: Cadogan, 2005.

Folley, Malcolm. *Monaco: Inside F1's Greatest Race*. London, England: Arrow Books, 2018.

Glatt, John. *The Royal House of Monaco*. New York, NY: St. Martin's Press, 2002.

McCulloch, Janelle. *Provence and the Cote d'Azur*. San Francisco, CA: Chronicle Books, 2015.

INDEX

INDEX